"I want to know your plans."

"Here's the deal, Carolyn. I don't have time to hold your hand and make sure you're happy with our investigation."

"Understood. But you need my help. Things are different on the ranch than in the city. People are different."

"I'm in charge. Get used to it," said Burke.

Carolyn's eyes narrowed. "Then we have a problem. I don't take orders. I will, however, respond to requests made with respect."

"You want me to say *please* and *thank-you?*"

"That's a start."

CASSIE MILES

COLORADO ABDUCTION

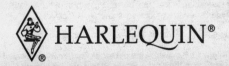

TORONTO • NEW YORK • LONDON
AMSTERDAM • PARIS • SYDNEY • HAMBURG
STOCKHOLM • ATHENS • TOKYO • MILAN • MADRID
PRAGUE • WARSAW • BUDAPEST • AUCKLAND

To the ever-encouraging Tess Foltz.
And, as always, to Rick.

Recycling programs
for this product may
not exist in your area.

ISBN-13: 978-0-373-88939-6

COLORADO ABDUCTION

www.eHarlequin.com

Printed in U.S.A.

ABOUT THE AUTHOR

Though born in Chicago and raised in L.A., Cassie Miles has lived in Colorado long enough to be considered a semi-native. The first home she owned was a log cabin in the mountains overlooking Elk Creek with a thirty-mile commute to her work at the *Denver Post*.

After raising two daughters and cooking tons of macaroni and cheese for her family, Cassie is trying to be more adventurous in her culinary efforts. Ceviche, anyone? She's discovered that almost anything tastes better with wine. A lot of wine. When she's not plotting Harlequin Intrigue books, Cassie likes to hang out at the Denver Botanical Gardens near her high-rise home.

Books by Cassie Miles

HARLEQUIN INTRIGUE
874—WARRIOR SPIRIT
904—UNDERCOVER COLORADO**
910—MURDER ON THE MOUNTAIN**
948—FOOTPRINTS IN THE SNOW
978—PROTECTIVE CONFINEMENT†
984—COMPROMISED SECURITY†
999—NAVAJO ECHOES
1025—CHRISTMAS COVER-UP
1048—MYSTERIOUS MILLIONAIRE
1074—IN THE MANOR WITH THE MILLIONAIRE
1102—CHRISTMAS CRIME IN COLORADO
1126—CRIMINALLY HANDSOME
1165—COLORADO ABDUCTION*

**Rocky Mountain Safe House
†Safe House: Mesa Verde
*Christmas at the Carlisles'

CAST OF CHARACTERS

J.D. Burke—Special agent for the FBI, he's a trained negotiator who's known for his skill in getting hostages released alive.

Carolyn Carlisle—The Denver-based CEO of Carlisle Certified Organic Beef, she grew up on the ranch near Delta and is capable of running both operations.

Dylan Carlisle—Carolyn's younger brother is the total cowboy. He's devastated by his wife's abduction.

Nicole Carlisle—Dylan's wife was in the wrong place at the wrong time.

Sheriff Trainer—The Delta County Sheriff is in way over his head with this investigation.

Polly Sanchez—Not only does she manage the cooking for the ranch hands but she's a comforting, maternal presence.

Jesse Longbridge—Founder of Longbridge Security, he defends Nicole with all his might and winds up in a coma.

Wentworth—Jesse's second in command.

Sam Logan—The charismatic founder of the SOF has a hand in several dangerous businesses, possibly including kidnapping.

SOF—Sons of Freedom.

Nate Miller—A lifelong enemy of the Carlisles, he owns the Circle M ranch, which is being rented by the SOF.

Lucas Mann—The foreman at the Carlisle Ranch has been part of the family for years.

Elvis—Carolyn's horse is all personality and carries a few extra pounds.

Chapter One

Too impatient to wait until the rotors of the helicopter came to a stop, Carolyn Carlisle disembarked, ducked and ran with her laptop in one hand and briefcase in the other. Dirt and dead leaves kicked up around her feet. Her long black hair whipped across her face. When she was in the clear, she gave the charter pilot a thumbs-up signal and the chopper took off, swooping through the Rocky Mountain sunset like a giant white dragonfly.

Silence returned to the wide valley, which sat in the shadow of snowcapped peaks. The surge of joy Carolyn usually felt when she returned to the cattle ranch where she'd grown up was absent. Her home, Carlisle Ranch, was under threat.

Last night, there was a fire at the north stable. Across the pasture, she could see the place where the barn once stood. The blackened ruin stood out in stark relief against the khaki-colored early December fields. The stench of burnt wood tainted the air. All the livestock had been rescued, thank God. But expensive equipment had been destroyed, and the sheriff suspected arson.

She marched up the walk toward a sprawling, two-story, whitewashed ranch house, originally built by her great-grandfather and added to by subsequent generations. Her first order of business was to kick her brother's butt for not calling her last night when the fire broke out.

Dylan had waited until today to inform her, probably because he didn't want her interfering. The family ranch, running about two thousand head of Angus, was his responsibility and he preferred that Carolyn stay in the Denver office of Carlisle Certified Organic Beef. Usually, their arrangement worked out well. She liked the city and loved the daily challenge of running a multimillion-dollar corporation.

But she was still a rancher at heart. As soon as she had heard about the stable fire, she'd had to be here. Hadn't even taken the time to change her business attire—teal silk blouse, black wool suit with a pencil skirt and high-heeled boots.

As she climbed the three stairs to the veranda that stretched across the front of the house, she was confronted by a cowboy with a rifle.

"Who are you?" she demanded.

"I work for Longbridge Security, ma'am." He pointed to a trefoil patch on the arm of his denim jacket.

"Did my brother Dylan hire you?"

"Yes, ma'am." He held open the front door for her.

She considered the presence of a bodyguard to be a good sign. At least Dylan was taking action. They couldn't really expect the Delta County sheriff's office to patrol the thousands of acres they leased for grazing.

Leaving her laptop and briefcase by the coatrack, she went down the hallway toward her brother's office. The door was ajar and she heard voices from inside—angry voices.

Her brother's wife of five years, Nicole, stormed from the room. Her blue eyes were furious. Her jaw clenched. "I'm sorry you had to hear that, Carolyn."

"I just got here." She liked and respected Nicole. Considered her more like a sister than a sister-in-law. "I was just getting ready to yell at Dylan myself."

"Be my guest."

"First, we could go out to the kitchen and have a cup of tea. Or something stronger if you like."

"Right now I just want to be alone." Nicole went to the front door. "I'm going to take a ride down by the creek."

The door slammed behind her.

Carolyn's first impulse was to follow her, but Dylan stepped into the hall. "How the hell did you get here so fast?"

"I chartered a chopper. After you finally got around to telling me about the fire, I wanted to see for myself that Elvis was all right."

"Your horse is fine. He's in the corral by the barn."

She'd intended to read him the riot act, but he already looked miserable. His shoulders slumped. His pale green eyes—identical to hers—were red-rimmed. "We need to talk."

"You missed Thanksgiving. Again."

"I had to work." And she wasn't going to let him guilt her out for shirking family responsibilities. Her every waking thought was devoted to running the family business. "What happened, Dylan? Was it arson?"

"There's nothing you can do." He stepped back into his office and shut the door.

Good old Western stoicism. Closed doors all around. *Never show emotion. Never share what's really wrong. Never ever cry.* That cowboy ethic might have worked in the Old West, but this was the twenty-first century with psychologists on every corner.

In search of a sympathetic ear, Carolyn left the house and headed toward the outdoor corral attached to the big barn with stables in the back. If she hurried, she could catch Nicole who was probably still getting saddled up. Instead, Carolyn looked for her version of a shrink. Elvis.

Reaching over the top rail of the corral, she stroked the white blaze on her horse's forehead. His upper lip curled in the trademark sneer of his namesake. He batted his long lashes, shamelessly flirting though he was over sixteen years old and had expanded his girth since she last saw him.

"No more sweets for you, Elvis."

He whinnied in protest.

She tugged a forelock of his black mane. "If you get any fatter, you won't fit into your white jumpsuit."

As she watched Nicole head out, Carolyn shivered. She should have grabbed a jacket before she came out, but the weather was pleasant enough—probably in the mid-fifties—and her blood still boiled with anger. She had a bad feeling about Nicole riding alone. It didn't seem safe. Not if there was an arsonist on the loose. A few minutes later, a man wearing a jacket with the Longbridge Security patch rode from the barn to follow her.

She turned her attention to Elvis. The horse listened while she talked about her worries about the ranch, about Dylan and Nicole. They'd always seemed like the perfect couple. If they couldn't make it, what hope did Carolyn have of finding a mate? She was thirty-three with no special man to warm her bed. Her last date had been a disaster and…

A noise distracted her. A snap that ricocheted across the valley. A rifle shot?

Carolyn peered across the field. The bodyguard and Nicole were nowhere in sight.

The grizzled ranch foreman, Lucas Mann, came around the corner of the barn, moving faster than his usual bowlegged saunter. "Carolyn, did you hear that?"

"Hush." She listened hard. A volley of shots echoed from far away, like pebbles being dropped in a metal bucket. Sound traveled great distances in the thin mountain air and she couldn't tell where the gunfire was coming from. "Lucas, give me your gun."

"What?"

"You heard me."

Lucas handed over his sidearm. Though he looked like an old-time cowboy, the weapon he carried in his belt holster was a brand-new Glock nine millimeter.

Carolyn tucked the gun into the waistband of her skirt. "We need to find Nicole and make sure she's okay. She was headed southwest toward the creek. I want you to saddle up. Bring one of those security guards."

"What the hell are you fixing to do?"

"Take care of business." If someone had fired on Nicole, she needed backup. And she needed it now.

In her high-heeled boots, Carolyn climbed the corral fence, tore the slit on her wool skirt and slung her leg over Elvis's bare back. As soon as Lucas unlatched the corral gate, she rode through. Digging her heels into Elvis's flanks, she took off across the field.

Riding without a saddle wasn't easy, especially not with the horse's bristly coat snagging her panty hose and an automatic pistol digging into her side. She wouldn't have attempted this ride with any other mount, but Elvis's gait was as familiar as her own jogging style. Her body adjusted instinctively to the rhythm of his gait. In her teens, she and Elvis had won dozens of trophies and blue ribbons for calf roping and barrel racing in local rodeos.

She clung to his mane and directed him with pressure from her knees and verbal commands. The chilly December wind sharpened her tension as she rode toward the area where the valley merged into rocky hillsides covered with forests of ponderosa pine.

She hadn't heard any other shots. If there had been a gunfight, it was over. The damage was done.

What if Nicole and the bodyguard were shot and bleeding? *Can't think about that now.* She needed to stay focused. *That's what I do best—hard-driving, straightforward action.*

Through the dusky gloom, she spotted a horseman coming out of the trees at a slow walk. The bodyguard. He slumped over his horse's neck. As his horse came to a stop, he slipped from the saddle to the ground.

She dismounted and ran toward the injured man. His shirt and denim jacket were covered in blood, his face twisted in pain. She sank to her knees beside him and pushed his jacket aside. If she could figure out where he'd been shot, she could apply pressure and slow the bleeding.

"Nicole." His voice was faint. "Couldn't save her."

Talking was too much of an effort. He needed to calm down and slow the pumping of his heart. But Carolyn had to ask, "Was she shot?"

"No." His eyelids closed. "They took her."

She tore open the buttons on his shirt, exposing a raw, gaping hole in his upper chest. Carolyn took off her suit jacket, wadded the fabric in a ball and pressed against the wound. Blood also stained the sleeve of his jacket and his leg. She had to get him to a hospital.

His hand gripped hers. He forced his eyes open and stared with fierce intensity. "Nicole tried to fight. Two men. One of them hit her. She fell. Didn't move."

Carolyn choked back a helpless sob. *Oh, God. How could this happen?*

"The other guy…" The bodyguard coughed. His fingers tightened. "He stood guard. He got off a shot. Before I could get close enough to…"

"You did the best you could."

"I fell off my horse. Couldn't move. Just lay there." It must have taken a fierce effort for him to mount up. Even now, he struggled to sit. "Saw their faces. I can ID them."

"Settle down." Though she respected his courage, this man wasn't going anywhere. "Help is on the way."

She glanced over her shoulder. What was taking so long? Lucas should have been here by now.

The bodyguard lay back. His chest heaved. Yet he forced himself to speak. "They said Dylan would pay. He'd pay a lot. To get his wife back."

"Are you telling me Nicole was kidnapped?"

"That's right. Kidnapped."

His eyes closed and his body went limp. He was still breathing. But just barely.

Her arms ached from putting pressure on his wound. The jacket she pressed against his chest was already soaked in blood. His chances for survival decreased with every minute.

"Don't die." Tears slid down her cheeks. "Please. Please, don't die."

She heard the sound of hoofbeats approaching and dashed away her tears. If the men found her crying, they wouldn't listen to a word she said. And Carolyn needed to take charge, needed to be strong. Her brother was going to be crazy and illogical— dangerously irrational.

The bodyguard she'd met on the veranda joined her on the ground beside the injured man. "I'll take it from here, ma'am. I'm a medic."

"He's unconscious."

"You did the right thing," he said, "putting pressure on the wound. Don't worry. We'll get him to the hospital."

She stood and stepped out of the way, relieved that the wounded bodyguard would be cared for by someone who knew what he was doing. Turning on the heel of her boot, she faced four other men on horseback. All of them had rifles. They looked like a posse from the Old West.

Lucas swung down from his horse and came toward her. "You've got blood all over. Are you hurt?"

"I'm okay."

"Where's Nicole?"

Her lips pinched together. If she told them Nicole had been kidnapped, they'd take off to rescue her. They were cowboys, experienced hunters who were capable of following the track of a jackrabbit across miles of mountain terrain. If they located the kidnappers, there'd be a shoot-out.

The paramedic called out. "I need the first-aid kit in my saddlebag. Somebody call an ambulance."

"You heard him," Carolyn said. "The first thing is to get this man to a hospital. He's lost a lot of blood."

While the other cowboys followed instructions from the paramedic, she saw her brother racing toward them, leaning low over the mane of his horse, riding like the demons of hell were on his tail. He pulled up and dismounted in a single move, hit the ground running and yanked her into a hug. "Thank God, you're all right."

"I'm fine." She could feel the tension in his body. Every muscle was clenched. Dylan wasn't going to like what she had to say, but there was no way to get around it.

His eyes were wild. "Where's Nicole?"

"Listen to me, Dylan." She grabbed his arm and held on tight, hoping she could save him from his own temper. "Before the bodyguard was shot, he saw two men with Nicole. He heard them say that you'd pay a lot to get your wife back. They kidnapped her."

He tore free from her grasp. "I'll kill the bastards."

Exactly what she was afraid of. "Think about what you're saying. If there's a gunfight, Nicole could be hurt."

He strode a few paces away from her, yanked off his hat and slapped it against his thigh. "What the hell am I supposed to do? Twiddle my thumbs while some son of a bitch holds my wife hostage? Wait for the sheriff to figure this out?"

"Let me handle this. The bodyguard who tried to protect Nicole is already standing at death's door. I don't want anybody else to get shot."

"She's my wife. I've got to find her."

Her brother was the most hardheaded man she'd ever known. There was no point in trying to talk sense into him. "I can see that I'm not going to change your mind."

"Hell no."

"Then give me your gun. I want all of your posse's guns. It can't hurt for you to track the kidnappers, but if you're not armed, you can't start a shoot-out."

"This isn't your call."

"Before Dad died, he told me to take care of my little brother. And that's what I intend to do."

He threw up his hands. "It's not fair to bring Dad's ghost into this situation."

She didn't play fair, she played to win. "Dad wouldn't want you to risk your life. Or anybody else's."

"Fine. We'll leave the guns. What are you going to do?"

"Go back to the house and wait to hear from the kidnappers." That wasn't enough and she knew it. "And I'm calling in the FBI."

TWO AND A HALF HOURS LATER, Carolyn stood on the veranda outside the house. The porch lights shone on a black van that had just parked next to the Delta County sheriff's SUV. This had to be the FBI.

A tall man emerged from the passenger seat.

Instead of the typical FBI black suit, he wore jeans and a worn leather jacket. As he strode toward her, he seemed to get even taller. He was probably six foot four. His sandy brown hair was less well-groomed than she'd expect from a federal agent, but he had an unmistakable air of authority—an attitude that immediately put her on edge.

"Special Agent J. D. Burke." He identified himself as he held up his badge. "I need to talk to the sheriff."

"Sheriff Trainer isn't here." At her urging, the sheriff had borrowed a horse and went to keep an eye on Dylan and his posse. She hoped the presence of a lawman might deter any attempt at vigilante justice.

"Who's in charge?"

Carolyn had changed from her bloodstained business clothes into jeans, a pink T-shirt and zippered hoodie. With her black hair pulled up in a ponytail, she probably didn't look like the top executive of a multimillion-dollar company. Still, she resented the way he looked right past her, trying to find a man in charge.

"I'm Carolyn Carlisle." She held out her hand. "I'm the boss."

When he shook her hand and made direct eye contact, she felt a jolt of electricity—a warning. His dark eyes were hard, implacable. She and this fed were going to butt heads.

"Have you heard from the kidnappers?" he asked.

"Not yet."

Three other men left the van and came toward the house. All were carrying equipment in black cases.

"We need to set up," Agent Burke said.

She held open the front door as they trooped through. "You can use the office. It's down the hall to the left."

Ignoring her words, he went past the staircase to the dining room with the long oak table. "This will do."

She hated the way he disregarded her suggestion, not even acknowledging her. Biting her lower lip, she held back her protest when his men pulled the chairs away from the table. Without a word to her, they opened their cases and began spreading out equipment—all kinds of electronics and computers.

He glanced over his shoulder at her. "We could use some coffee."

His arrogance astounded her. "I'll bet you could."

"I take mine black."

The last straw. No way would she be relegated to the position of fetching coffee.

"Listen to me, Agent Burke." She struggled to keep from snarling. "I called in the FBI. As far as I'm concerned, you owe me an explanation of what you're doing."

"Yeah, sure."

"You," she snapped, "work for me."

Chapter Two

The razor edge in her voice caused Burke to turn and face this slim-hipped woman in cowboy boots. Anger blew off her like a hurricane.

"This is my ranch. My house." Her tone was sharp but controlled. "I insist upon being treated with respect. I'm not your errand girl. I don't bring you coffee. I don't tidy up after you. And I demand to know what's going on."

She looked like a teenager, but there was nothing girlish about her temper. Carolyn Carlisle was a mature and formidable woman.

He peered into her eyes. They were fascinating, with green irises so pale they were almost transparent. She stared back at him, hard and determined, as she waited for his answer.

"What do you want to know, Carolyn?" He purposefully used her first name to establish that he was the professional and she was a civilian.

"Well, J.D…." When she countered immediately

with his first name, he almost grinned. This woman didn't miss a beat.

"Actually," he said, "I go by Burke."

"Okay, Burke. I want an explanation of all this equipment you've scattered across my dining room table. But first, I want to know your plans."

"Here's the deal, Carolyn. I don't have time to hold your hand and make sure you're happy with our investigation. I didn't come here to make friends."

"Understood. But you need my help. Things are different on the ranch than in the city. People are different."

As far as he was concerned, a criminal was a criminal. Their motivations and methods might change from place to place, but the underlying stupidity and cruelty were a constant. "This is a crisis situation and I'm in charge. That's the way it rolls. Get used to it."

Her fascinating eyes narrowed. "Get used to what?"

"I give the orders."

"Then we have a problem. I don't take orders. I will, however, respond to requests made with respect."

"You want me to say please and thank you?"

"That's a start."

Her smile was infuriating and at the same time attractive. Even sexy. If they had met under different circumstances, he might have pursued her. But not here. Not now. As a hostage negotiator, he knew better than to become emotionally invested. The survival rate for kidnap victims held for ransom within the United States was less than forty percent. Nicole's abduction probably wasn't going to end well.

The phone on the table rang. "This could be the kidnappers."

Carolyn's bravado vanished. "What do I do?"

"It's on speakerphone," Burke said. "If it's the kidnappers, you need to keep them talking and demand to speak to Nicole."

He pressed a button and gave her a nod.

"Hello," she said. "Carolyn Carlisle speaking."

"Yes, ma'am. This is Wentworth. I wanted to give you an update."

Her tension relaxed. "I have you on speaker-phone, Wentworth. I'm here with the FBI. We're waiting to hear from the kidnappers."

"Who is he?" Burke asked.

"One of the security guards my brother hired. Wentworth is at the hospital with the wounded man, Jesse Longbridge, the owner of the security company." She turned back toward the speaker. "How is he?"

"In critical condition," said the voice on the phone. "His heart stopped during surgery. He hasn't regained consciousness, but he's breathing on his own."

"Is he going to be okay?" Carolyn asked.

"It's touch and go, ma'am."

She wrapped her arms around her midsection as if literally holding herself together. To Burke she said, "Jesse saw the kidnappers. He can identify them as soon as he wakes up."

If he wakes up. He leaned toward the phone. "We appreciate the update, Wentworth. This is Special Agent J. D. Burke of the FBI. Can you call in another man from your security company?"

"Yes, sir."

"Good. I want two of you at the hospital, keeping an eye on Jesse Longbridge. He's a threat to the kidnappers and they might come after him."

"We'll keep him safe, sir."

Burke recognized the crisp attitude. "Are you former military, Wentworth?"

"Marine Corps. Two tours of duty in Iraq as a medic."

There was no need for further conversation. Burke had complete confidence in Wentworth's ability to keep the witness safe. The first lesson for a Marine was never leave a man behind. "Carry on, Wentworth."

"And thank you," Carolyn added before he hung up.

He figured that the veneer of politeness she insisted upon was a way to maintain control. It was a small price to pay for her cooperation. "Carolyn, would you please tell us the events leading up to the kidnapping."

She gave a brief nod. "It was dusk. Nicole went for a ride. She wanted to be alone, but the bodyguard, Jesse, left a few minutes later. I heard shots and went after them."

"How long between when they left and when you heard gunshots?"

"Maybe ten minutes."

"Did you pursue on foot?"

"On horse. Bareback. I happened to be near the corral." She frowned. "I wasn't dressed for riding, and I ruined a perfectly good skirt. Tore the slit all the way up the side."

His mind formed an image of her long legs pressed against the flanks of her horse as she raced across the field. It must have been something to see. "Then what happened?"

"I saw Jesse coming out of the trees. Even though he was badly wounded, he managed to tell me that ☰☰ two men grab Nicole. She struggled, but ☰☰cked her unconscious. They said that my ☰☰ould pay a lot to get his wife back."

☰☰tly, this wasn't a planned abduction. ☰☰ no way the kidnappers could have ☐icole would be out riding at that particu-☰ent. Not unless she was part of their plan. ☰t were so, she wouldn't have struggled, wouldn't have needed to be rendered unconscious.

More likely, this was a crime of opportunity. Nicole happened to be in the wrong place at the wrong time.

Bad news. Burke preferred to deal with professional criminals. Amateurs were unpredictable. "What happened next?"

"The men from the ranch rode up. Wentworth took care of Jesse. And he was nothing short of amazing. He got Jesse loaded into the bed of a truck and took him to the hospital before the ambulance arrived."

Jesse Longbridge had been lucky to have the battle-trained expertise of a Marine medic. Wentworth's fast action and triage skills had probably saved his life.

"After that," Carolyn said, "I had to deal with my brother, Dylan. He wanted to track down the kidnappers and kill them. But I insisted that all the men leave their guns behind. The sheriff is with them now. They're still looking, talking to people at nearby ranches."

Burke needed to put an end to this chase as possible. He strode from the room.

"Where are you going?" she asked.

"To get us some coffee. It's going to night."

NEAR ELEVEN O'CLOCK, Carolyn paced bac forth on the veranda, waiting anxiously for her brother to return. After half a dozen calls on her cell phone, she'd finally convinced him to allow the FBI to handle the kidnapping. Even if Burke was a pain in the rear, he was an expert.

The equipment he'd finally deigned to show her was impressive: GPS surveillance, heat-sensing infrared imaging, audio scanners, computer linkups to monitor e-mail activity. These high-tech tools made her brother's posse on horseback seem positively archaic.

She knew Dylan would be impressed by the technology. The problem was Burke. If he tried to order her brother around, there'd be hell to pay.

Her first impression of Burke as a brusque, authoritative jerk had changed. He'd shown patience when he'd explained how to handle the ransom call. He'd told her not to confront but to stand firm. And to keep the caller talking. There were two reasons for that strategy. First, so they could get a clear trace. Second, the more the kidnapper talked, the more information they could gather. Little sounds in the background were clues to the kidnapper's whereabouts.

Burke and his men had practiced with her so she'd know what to say. They'd told her to use her feminine wiles to stall—a useless bit of advice. If she'd ever had wiles, they were buried under years of dealing with ranch hands and businessmen who didn't respect a woman who cried or pouted or giggled.

According to the FBI experts, her number one goal when talking to the kidnappers was to get proof of life.

She shuddered when she thought of the alternative. Nicole could already be dead. Her fingers tightened on the porch banister, anchoring her to something solid and tangible.

Burke came onto the porch and stood beside her. The sheer size of the man was impressive. He stood well over six feet tall with long legs and wide shoulders. She couldn't really guess at his age, but assumed that a senior FBI agent would be in his late thirties. A little older than she was.

"Are you chilly?" he asked.

"Not a bit." She stuck her hands into the fur-lined pockets of the hip-length shearling jacket that protected her from the December cold.

"It's beautiful out here," he said. "Peaceful."

"When I was growing up, I couldn't wait to get off the ranch. After I left, I kept wanting to come back."

"But you live in Denver now. Tell me about your job." He paused for a moment. "Please."

"You've asked so nicely, I can't refuse."

She glanced up, catching a twinkle in his dark brown eyes. Though he was willing to play along with her insistence for respect, he made it clear that the decision was his choice. He was still in charge.

His attitude was familiar. All her life she'd been dealing with taciturn, stubborn men. Cowboys weren't known for wearing their hearts on their sleeves unless you put a guitar in their hands. A mournful tune could bring sentimental tears to the eyes of the most calloused ranch hand.

She strolled to the end of the veranda, climbed onto the porch swing and tucked her legs under her.

"My job," she said. "I'm the CEO at Carlisle Certified Organic Beef. I handle oversight of the product, sales and distribution for this ranch and more than sixty others throughout the west. Anybody who contracts with us agrees to follow sustainable ranching procedures that my father pioneered in the 1980s. All Carlisle Certified cattle are grass fed. We don't use antibiotics or growth hormones."

"With the craze for organic food, you must be doing well."

"The business keeps me hopping, and we're also doing something good for the planet. Our system of shifting cattle from field to field prevents overgrazing. I like to think that we have a contented herd."

"But they still get slaughtered."

She leaned forward, setting the swing into motion. The chain that attached to hooks in the porch ceiling creaked. "I hate to think about that part. For a long time I was a vegetarian."

"On a ranch?"

"Don't even think about giving me a hard time. I've heard it all." She swung a little harder. "Currently, we have plans to build a state-of-the-art, humane slaughterhouse a couple of miles from here."

"I can't get a handle on you." He regarded her with curiosity. "Are you a hard-driving businesswoman? Or a tree-hugging environmentalist?"

"A little bit of both. I try to avoid politics."

He sauntered toward her and sank into a sturdy, carved rocking chair beside the swing. "I'd find that statement easier to believe if the FBI hadn't been alerted to Nicole's kidnapping by the governor's office."

She hadn't wanted to waste time going through regular law enforcement channels. "The governor is a friend. I called in a favor."

"But you're not political."

She didn't need to justify her position to him. What an *irritating man!* "Why do you want to know about my job?"

"Motivation," he said. "I'm trying to figure out who has a grudge against you or your brother. For the past couple of weeks, somebody has been causing a lot of trouble at the ranch."

"Trouble?" Dylan hadn't mentioned anything until today when he told her about the stable fire. "Please explain."

"I read the police reports your brother filed. Uprooted fence posts. Damage to the irrigation system in the hay field. A couple of pieces of stolen equipment." He leaned forward, elbows resting on his knees, and peered at her through the dim light. "You didn't know."

"These incidents sound like minor mischief. Dylan probably didn't want to worry me." Still, he should have kept her informed. It seemed like he didn't trust her anymore. What was wrong with him? He'd never been secretive. Before today, she'd never heard him fight with Nicole.

"It was more than mischief," Burke said. "Sounds like deliberate sabotage at the ranch. Have there been any threats on the corporate side?"

"Not that I'm aware of. Of course, we have competitors. And disgruntled former employees. But that kind of hostility usually shows up in the form of a lawsuit."

She heard the sounds of horsemen approaching and saw the posse riding toward the barn. Slowly, she uncurled her legs and stood, watching. Dylan handed his reins to one of the other ranch hands and strode toward them. With his head down and his face shadowed by the brim of his Stetson, she couldn't see his expression. But she knew he was troubled. His gait was stiff-legged, not surprising for someone who'd been on horseback for several hours.

He had to be devastated about the kidnapping. No matter how much she wanted to ask him why he hadn't told her about the sabotage, now wasn't the right time.

Dylan stepped onto the veranda. He pulled off his leather gloves and his hat, dropping them on a rocking chair. His matted black hair stuck to the sides of his head. His complexion was red and raw from exposure to the cold night air.

"Dylan, I want you to meet Special Agent J. D. Burke."

The two men faced off as they shook hands. Burke was taller and broader, but Dylan was clearly the aggressor.

"You find my wife," he said. "I want a search helicopter. First thing in the morning. And bloodhounds. Hell, I want you to call out the National Guard. And I—"

"Dylan," Carolyn interrupted. "What did you find when you were tracking?"

"They went across the back ridge to a paved road. We lost their track. We've been going door-to-door at the nearby ranches. Nobody's seen anything. Not a damn thing."

One of Burke's men pushed open the door. "Carolyn, it's the phone."

"The kidnappers," Dylan said. "I'll take that call."

"No," she said. "You won't. I've been practicing. I know what to say."

When he started toward the door, Burke stepped in front of him. "Let Carolyn handle this."

"Like hell I will."

She slipped inside and ran to answer the phone before Dylan could do anything to stop her.

Chapter Three

Burke would have preferred being inside, listening while Carolyn talked to the kidnappers. But he knew his men would record the conversation. During the next few hours, they'd replay it a hundred times, doing voice analysis and isolating every miniscule background noise.

Right now, it was more important to hold Dylan back. Burke wouldn't hesitate to kick this cowboy's ass to keep him from barging in and botching their procedures. He stood in front of Dylan like a brick wall.

"Let me pass." Dylan seemed dazed, in shock. His pale green eyes—the same color as Carolyn's—flickered nervously. "I need to be in there."

Burke didn't waste time on logical explanations. He doubted Dylan Carlisle could hear anything other than the roar of outrage inside his head. It must be an all-consuming noise, louder than an avalanche.

"We're staying out here," Burke said.

"She's my wife."

"I understand." If Burke had allowed himself to become emotionally involved with the people on a case, he would have felt sorry for this guy.

"My wife…" His voice cracked. "I love her."

Though Burke hadn't touched him, Dylan staggered backward a few paces. The air deflated from his lungs in a gush of cold vapor. He turned, facing the night sky. His fingers gripped the banister. "We had a fight. Right before she rode off by herself, we argued. I said things. Hurtful things."

Burke stepped up beside him but didn't look at him. He stood silently, listening like a priest in a confessional.

"Nicole wants a baby." The words spilled from Dylan as if he'd been holding everything inside for too long. "We've been trying for eight or nine months. But no luck. From the start, we knew she might have to be implanted because she had internal injuries from when she got kicked by a horse a couple of years ago. Kind of an occupational hazard, I guess. She's a large animal veterinarian."

Burke heard the pride in his voice. Dylan truly loved his wife.

He continued, "She's a tiny little thing. But tough. First time I saw her, she stuck her arm into a cow's birthing canal and pulled a slick, wet, newborn calf into the world." He shook his head.

Something like a sob came through his lips. "You've got to love a woman like that."

That wasn't Burke's number one criteria, but he understood. "She was right for you."

"We were supposed to go to the fertility doctor today. He'd scheduled the implant procedure. But I couldn't go. Not with the stable fire. I had to be here."

Actually, he could have called Carolyn. She was more than able to manage the ranch while Dylan was at the doctor with his wife. Burke guessed that something else was going on. Maybe Dylan wasn't ready for kids.

He continued, "I told her we could do it tomorrow or the next day. Why did it have to happen today? What difference could one day make?"

A big difference. It took less than a day to change someone's life. Sometimes, less than a minute.

Carolyn pushed open the door and stepped onto the veranda. She trembled. "A million-dollar ransom. He wants it by tomorrow afternoon."

THE SOUND OF THE KIDNAPPER'S voice set fire to a fuse inside Carolyn. She was furious. And terrified. They had to rescue Nicole. *Now, damn it. Right now.*

But there were procedures to follow, and she trusted Burke's expertise. He moved around the dining room, checking the various instruments and conferring with his men in technical jargon that sounded like a foreign language.

Needing something to do, she picked up Burke's leather jacket from the dining room chair where he'd dropped it. The lining was still warm from his body heat. He glanced in her direction. Was he smirking? In spite of her earlier insistence that she wasn't an errand girl, she'd been reduced to tidying up. Immediately, Carolyn dropped the jacket and stood tall, arms folded below her breasts.

Sheriff Trainer had joined them. The only other person in the room was her brother. Dylan leaned against the wall by the door, near collapse.

"We're going to play back the ransom call," Burke said. "I want you all to listen for any sound that might give us a clue to the kidnapper's identity or his whereabouts."

"Wait a minute," Sheriff Trainer said. "Didn't you get a trace to tell us where he is?"

One of Burke's associates, Special Agent Corelli, stepped forward. He was the technical expert, the only man in the room wearing a suit and tie. He pointed to a rectangular black box with several dials. On the screen was a map of the area. A red dot blinked on a secluded road, too small to be given a name.

Corelli pointed to the dot. "When he made the

call, he was here. I'd guess that he's on horseback or in an all-terrain vehicle."

Dylan staggered forward and squinted at the screen. "Does he have Nicole with him?"

"Sorry," Corelli said. "There's no way of knowing."

Carolyn went to her brother's side. "Sit down, Dylan."

"Can't." He stumbled back to his position against the wall. "If I sit, I'll fall asleep."

"That sounds like a good idea."

"I won't sleep until Nicole is in the bed beside me."

A noble sentiment. But it wouldn't do Nicole any good if he pushed himself beyond his limits and had a total breakdown.

The sheriff tilted his hat back on his head and stared at the blinking dot. Though he wasn't holding a cigarette, Carolyn smelled the residual smoke that clung to his uniform. "Seems to me that we ought to head out in that direction."

"He'll be long gone," Burke said. "He was smart enough to know that the phone call would be traced. He's in a remote area with no witnesses. There's no way we could have gotten there in time. He used a disposable cell phone so we can't ID the number."

"There are still records of those things," the sheriff said. "We can find out where he bought it."

"We're running those records," Corelli said.

Carolyn was surprised that the Delta County sheriff was so attuned to complex investigation techniques. She'd always thought the skinny, gray-haired man was a nice guy, but not particularly competent.

"The good news," Burke said, "is that our kidnapper is still in the area. More than likely, he's a local. Somebody you might know. That's why I want you to listen to his voice. And the way he puts his words together."

He pressed the playback button and Carolyn heard her own voice. She was surprised that she didn't sound as terrified as she'd felt at the time.

"Hello, this is Carolyn Carlisle."

"I want a million dollars." The kidnapper spoke in a rasping, ominous, barely audible whisper. "I want it in cash."

"You'll have to repeat that. I can't hear you." She'd been stalling, doing as Burke had suggested. "Please speak up."

"Listen hard. A million dollars. Cash. Nothing bigger than a hundred."

"Do you have Nicole with you? I need to talk to her."

"Pay me. Or she dies."

On the playback Carolyn sounded confident. "Don't you worry. You'll get everything you want. If it's a million dollars, you'll get a million." She'd been rambling, keeping him on the line. "Please let me talk to Nicole."

"I want the money tomorrow afternoon at five."

"It's going to be hard to scrape that much cash together in one day." More stalling. "Tomorrow is Saturday. And the local banks probably don't have a million dollars on hand. We'll have to go all the way into Denver."

"Not my problem."

She remembered Corelli giving her the thumbs-up signal. They had successfully made the trace.

She heard herself say, "I need proof of life."

There was a pause. "What's that?"

"Proof that Nicole is still alive. Let me talk to her."

"You'll get your proof."

That was when he disconnected the call.

She looked into Dylan's face. Tears streaked down his cheeks. Carolyn couldn't remember the last time she'd seen her brother cry. When she touched his arm, he collapsed against her.

"This is all going to work out," she assured him. "I'll take care of putting the money together."

Burke cleared his throat. "Anybody recognize the voice?"

"Not really." The sheriff patted the pocket in his shirt where Carolyn could see the outline of a cigarette pack. "That whisper could have been anybody. I didn't hear an accent. He didn't use any slang."

"Proper language," Burke said. "Instead of saying 'Ain't my problem' he said 'Not my problem.' And he didn't know what proof of life meant."

"What does that indicate?" Carolyn asked.

"He's not a professional kidnapper. He might not even have a criminal record."

"Which means," Corelli said, "that his finger-prints might not be in the system."

Burke nodded toward the other two men, both of whom were wearing black windbreakers with *FBI* stenciled across the back. "Special Agent Smith and Special Agent Silverman are both trained pro-filers. Sheriff, they're going to need to talk to every-body on the ranch. Starting now."

"It's the middle of the night," the sheriff pro-tested.

"The first twenty-four hours are crucial." Burke turned to the Smith–Silverman team. "Start your interviews with the sheriff. Keep me informed."

Carolyn could feel Dylan's knees beginning to buckle. His body was literally giving out. Before he went limp and dragged them both to the floor, Burke came up beside her and slipped his arm around Dylan's torso. "Let's go, buddy. You need a rest."

He tried to rally. "Can't go to bed."

"Just a catnap," Carolyn said. "On the sofa in your office. You'll be close."

With Burke supporting her brother, she went down the hall, through the entryway, and took a right. The second door was Dylan's office—a large, masculine room with a wall of books and windows that opened onto the veranda. Opposite the huge oak desk that had belonged to her father were two brown leather chairs and a matching sofa.

Burke sat Dylan on the sofa, and Carolyn peeled off his jacket. Getting his boots off was an effort but she managed. Her brother stretched out, immediately asleep. She covered him with a crocheted afghan, striped in green and brown.

Closing the door, she stepped into the hallway with Burke. "Thanks. I couldn't have carried him by myself. Whoever said 'He ain't heavy, he's my brother,' didn't know Dylan."

"The Hollies," Burke said. "They sang it."

She leaned against the wall outside the office, allowing this moment of quiet to soothe her frazzled nerves. It was nice to be here with Burke—someone who didn't depend on her. "I'm worried about him."

"Dylan blames himself for what happened." His voice was low, intimate. "He and Nicole argued before she took off."

"I heard them." That was less than six hours ago but it felt like an eternity. "I didn't catch what they were saying."

"They were trying to get pregnant. Your brother

didn't want to take time out of his schedule to see the fertility doctor. That's why Nicole was angry."

"Dylan told you all that?" She gazed up into his stern, craggy face. In the soft light, his features seemed warmer, more appealing. "If I can't get him to open up to me, why would he talk to you?"

"Sometimes, it's easier to tell your secrets to a stranger."

Unexpectedly, he reached toward her and brushed a loose strand of hair behind her ear. The stroke of his fingertips on her cheek set off an electric reaction that sizzled down her throat and into her chest. "You don't seem all that strange. Actually, you're kind of all right."

"High praise," he said wryly. "Don't make me more than I am, Carolyn. I'm just doing my job."

She didn't quite believe him. Burke tried to stay detached, but the hard-nosed attitude didn't come naturally. "You're not as tough as you pretend to be. You care about what happens to Nicole. And to Dylan."

"Caring is human. But I don't let empathy get in the way of my work."

"I don't mean to put you on the spot. It's just—"

"And I care about you," he said.

Her heart thumped against her rib cage. Her gaze dropped from his face to his broad chest. Just for a moment, she wished she could rest her head against him. "Thank you."

"You're trying to carry your brother, run the corporate business and manage the ranch." He rested one hand on her shoulder. With the other, he lifted her chin so she was looking into his dark eyes. "Who takes care of you, Carolyn?"

No one. She had no one to share her burdens. No one who really cared for her. "I talk to Elvis."

His lips parted in a grin. "First the Hollies. Now Elvis. Are we on a tour of the golden oldies?"

"Elvis is my horse. I tell him my secrets and he listens."

Burke leaned down and kissed her forehead. He stepped back so quickly that she wasn't sure what happened. But her forehead tingled. She felt suddenly warm. Hot even.

One of the other agents—either Silverman or Smith—came into the hallway. "Burke, you need to hear this."

"What is it?"

"The sheriff says the most likely suspects live on a ranch near here. The Circle M."

Burke turned to Carolyn. "What do you know about the Circle M?"

"The ranch belongs to Nate Miller, but he's renting the entire property and all the outbuildings to Sam Logan and a group of his followers."

"Followers?"

"They call themselves the sons of something or other. They're survivalists."

Burke looked back toward the other agent. He said just one word. "Waco."

In a flash she remembered television images of burning buildings and reporters talking about the women and children who had died in the confrontation between the FBI and the Waco cult.

"It's not the same thing," she said quickly. "Sam Logan isn't that kind of guy."

"How do you know?" Burke asked.

She swallowed hard. "He used to be my boyfriend."

Chapter Four

Sam Logan hadn't been the love of Carolyn's life. He'd been two years ahead of her in high school, and they went out on exactly three dates before he told her that she wasn't "sophisticated" enough for him. In his dictionary, "sophisticated" meant having sex, which wasn't something she wanted to try at age sixteen.

Several years later, after she'd graduated from college, she and Logan hooked up again. Their relationship had been far more complicated the second time around.

"Well?" Burke glared at her as if she were a suspect. "Are you going to tell us about your survivalist boyfriend?"

"I need coffee for this."

She pivoted and went down the hall toward the kitchen where the family's housekeeper, Polly Sanchez, was taking a batch of her famous raisin rolls out of the oven. The heat from her baking steamed up the north-facing windows. A mouthwatering aroma filled the huge kitchen.

"Can I help?" Carolyn asked.

"Good heavens, no. I'm in a hurry, and I don't have time to clean up after you." With an expert flourish, Polly spread gooey icing on top of the rolls. "Soon as I'm done here, I'm heading home to catch a couple of winks before morning."

As Carolyn watched the icing melt into rich swirls she realized that she hadn't eaten for over ten hours, not since noon when she had sushi from the new Japanese fusion restaurant down the street from her Denver office. Lunchtime seemed like decades ago.

She rested her hand on Polly's round shoulder. "Thanks for coming over to help out."

Beneath her curly gray hair, Polly's forehead crinkled with worry wrinkles. "You know I'd do anything for your family."

For the past twelve years, Polly had worked at the ranch as housekeeper and chief cook. Her husband, Juan, had been a full-time ranch hand—and an expert at repairing machinery—until three years ago when he was stricken with MS. Now, his hands were too weak and unsure to hold a wrench. As soon as she'd learned of his illness, Carolyn authorized payment for a full pension and upped Juan's medical coverage to pay for treatment. She'd offered to do the same for Polly so she could stay home with Juan, but the buxom little woman insisted that she needed to keep busy.

During the spring calving and fall roundup when they had a full crew, Polly had two employees working under her. At this time of year, her schedule was less demanding.

"You need me here," Polly said in a brisk tone. "Tomorrow morning, Juan and I will move over here to the ranch house, and we'll stay until Nicole comes home."

"That's really not necessary," Carolyn said.

"Honey, you've got a houseful of FBI agents and bodyguards. And you can't hardly boil water without setting the house afire. How did you plan to feed all these hungry men?"

"I can call for pizza."

"Pizza for breakfast?" Polly clucked her tongue on the roof of her mouth. "Y'all sit right here at the kitchen table. I'll bring your coffee and raisin rolls."

Taking the seat opposite Burke, Carolyn knew that the time had come to answer his question. "Okay, here's what happened between me and Sam Logan."

"Logan?" Polly set mugs of coffee on the table. "He's turned into a regular nutcase. He runs that Sons of Freedom bunch over at the Circle M. It's not all Sons. There are families. The women all wear house-dresses and tie their hair back. Same with the kids."

Burke turned toward her. "Is it a religious group?"

"Lord, no." Polly bustled back to the counter. "Logan doesn't have a religious bone in his body. Does he, Carolyn?"

"Not when we were going out." She remembered Sam Logan as a tall, lean guy with a blond ponytail and a charming smile—handsome enough to cruise by on his looks. She wasn't surprised that he'd gathered followers.

"His group," Polly said, "wants to go back to the pioneer days. They're against big business, government interference, taxation without representation and all that."

Burke shrugged. "Doesn't sound so bad to me."

His comment surprised Carolyn. What kind of fed was opposed to government interference? She'd thought FBI agents couldn't wait to bust down doors and take everybody into custody.

Polly placed a plate full of raisin rolls on the table. "People around here call them SOF for Sons of Freedom. Or Silly Old Fools. If the only thing they wanted was to go back to the good old days, I wouldn't have a problem with them. Live and let live, I always say."

"But you have a problem," Burke said. "What is it?"

She reached behind her back to untie the strings of the gingham apron she wore over her jeans and cotton shirt. "Their back-to-nature ideas don't extend to alcohol. A couple of the SOF boys drove into Riverdale, drunk as skunks, and raised hell. A local teenager got hurt. The sheriff could tell you more."

Carolyn bit into her raisin roll and let the gooey sweetness melt in her mouth.

"How do they support themselves?"

"Lord knows where they get their money. But they seem to have plenty. Nate Miller didn't rent out his land for cheap, that's for dang sure."

Carolyn glanced over at Burke who seemed totally focused on devouring his raisin roll. His dark eyes took on a glaze of contentment. His jaw relaxed as he chewed. The other FBI agent was likewise transported.

"These are great," Burke said. "Ma'am, you've got to come back tomorrow."

Polly pinched his cheek. *Actually pinched Burke's cheek!* Carolyn couldn't believe that Special Agent I'm-In-Charge would stand for such familiarity. Then she remembered his kiss on her forehead. Underneath the tough exterior, he was kind of a marshmallow.

"I'll be back in time to throw together some breakfast." Polly turned to Carolyn. "The guest bedrooms are made up with fresh sheets and towels. Call me if you need anything else tonight. G'night, y'all."

She headed out of the kitchen toward the front door.

"Nice woman," Burke said. "Must have been

good for you to have Polly around while you were growing up. She's real motherly."

"I have a mother," Carolyn said quickly. "Her name is Andrea. She and my father divorced when I was seven."

"Does she live around here?"

Thinking of her stylish mother choosing to stay in rural Colorado amused Carolyn. "Not hardly. She runs an art gallery in Manhattan where she lives with her second husband and my twelve-year-old half sister."

"Big change in lifestyle."

"Yeah, she traded in her cowgirl boots for designer stilettos."

Carolyn regretted that she hadn't spent more time with her mom when she was growing up. Andrea had wanted to take her and Dylan with her when she left, but they both chose the ranch. It was their home, their heritage. "I should call Mom and tell her what's going on."

"Tomorrow is soon enough," Burke said.

He was probably right. There was nothing her mother could do from New York, and Carolyn had more pressing concerns for tonight. "I need to get on the phone with my financial officers. And my bankers. I've got to start putting together the money for the kidnappers. Maybe I should—"

"Later," Burke said. "First, I want to know more about Sam Logan."

"Like what?" The sugar rush from Polly's raisin rolls had energized her. The inside of her head churned with dozens of things she needed to handle ASAP. "There's not much to tell."

"When you broke up with him were there hard feelings?"

"Some," she admitted. "It was a long time ago, right after grad school. I'd come back to the ranch and I was trying to figure out what I wanted to do with my pretty new MBA."

For lack of any other plan, she'd started dating Logan, who was a great guy to party with— handsome, charming and sexy. When their relationship started to get serious, she was uncomfortable. Her father, who had been ailing, sided with Logan, telling Carolyn it was high time she settled down.

But she'd just returned from school in New York where she had a chance to watch her career-focused mother. The corporate lifestyle appealed to Carolyn, and she figured she had the rest of her life to make babies. Now, almost ten years later, she wondered if she'd waited too long.

"Logan wasn't the right guy for me." She exhaled a sigh. "And I wasn't the barefoot-and-pregnant type of woman he was looking for."

"Do you think he holds a grudge?"

Taken aback, she grasped what he was suggesting. "If you think Logan kidnapped Nicole to get back at me, you're wrong. His ego is too big to realize that I was dumping him as much as he was dumping me."

"He could be nursing bad feelings toward you."

True, her former boyfriend had a petty streak. "He wouldn't sabotage the ranch. Our cattle-raising process is natural and organic. We're not his enemy."

"Are you sure about that?" Burke raised an eyebrow. "Carlisle Ranch is an international corporation. Big business. That's what he hates."

Burke's logic made a certain amount of sense. The success of her family's business might be a slap in the face to a loser like Sam Logan.

IT WAS AFTER MIDNIGHT when Burke and his men completed their interrogations of the employees of Carlisle Ranch. Once these cowboys got talking, they were as gossipy as a bunch of hens with ruffled feathers.

Burke still didn't have much to go on. Only a basic assumption: the kidnapping had been unpremeditated and was related to the recent vandalism at the ranch.

On a wide-screen computer in the dining room, Agent Corelli had pinpointed those acts of sabotage on a map of the area. Most of them bunched along the border between the Carlisles and a neighboring ranch.

Corelli, whose black suit still looked crisp, pointed to the red dots. "That pattern can't be a co-incidence. Who lives on that ranch?"

"A young widow and her four-year-old child." Not likely suspects for a brutal kidnapping. "It's not a working ranch. Less than a hundred acres."

"Who's next to her?"

"National Forest," Burke said. "There are a couple of oil rigs in that area but nobody lives there."

Logan's compound was across the road and further to the east. Burke considered the survival-ists his most likely suspects. They were the only ranch who had refused to talk to Dylan's posse when they had made their search.

Burke needed to get inside the SOF compound. His gut told him Logan had something to hide.

He stepped away from the table and stretched, trying to ease the tension that knotted the muscles in his neck and shoulders. "We need continuous monitoring tonight. In case the kidnappers call again," he said. "We'll sleep in shifts. You three go first. Silverman, I'll see you at three-thirty to relieve me."

Stretching again, he watched his men troop out of the command central/dining room. Upstairs, Polly had prepared two guest rooms for them with two beds in each. Twin-sized beds were always too short for Burke, but it would have felt good to lie flat, even with his feet dangling off the end of the bed.

In the living room that adjoined the dining room, he'd spotted a big, beige, corduroy easy chair with a matching ottoman. He hauled the chair around to face the battery of equipment on the table and settled in.

The house was quiet but not peaceful. The anxiety of waiting—not knowing what had happened to a loved one—permeated the old walls. The creaking of floorboards reminded him of the crackle of a long fuse, burning slowly toward an explosion. More trouble was coming; he could feel it.

Years ago, when he had started in law enforcement as a street cop in Chicago, he'd learned to trust his gut feelings. Subsequent training with the FBI gave him the tools to analyze.

Eyes half-closed, he did a risk assessment. Two violent crimes—arson and kidnapping—had occurred within two days. If he assumed that the same perpetrators were responsible for both, it was unlikely there would be another attack tonight. Typically, there was a lull after kidnappers made their ransom demands.

He heard a rustling from the hallway and turned his head with his eyelids still drooping. Carolyn entered the dining room, cell phone in hand. When she saw him, she stared for a moment as if deciding whether to wake him. Wispy strands of black hair had come undone from her ponytail. Though she fidgeted, she still looked capable. *And damned attractive.*

Her hidden vulnerability appealed to him. Behind her facade, he caught glimpses of a touching innocence that made him want to gather her into his arms and promise her the world. Which still didn't excuse him for kissing her forehead. He wasn't usually so unprofessional, but he didn't regret that kiss. Her skin tasted spicy—warm and soft.

"What do you need?" he asked.

She started. "I thought you were asleep."

"Just resting."

"I have a question."

"Shoot."

She placed her cell phone down on the table and approached him. "What if I can't put together the ransom by the deadline?"

He'd prefer that she not pay ransom at all. "Problems?"

"We don't have a million dollars in liquid assets, so the ransom requires a loan against our collateral, which, in turn, requires a ton of paperwork. Also, my financial adviser tells me that the local banks, even in Delta, can't pull that much cash from their reserves. We'll have to use a Denver bank and fly the money over here."

"I'm impressed that you found out that much tonight."

"I get things done, Burke."

She wasn't bragging, just stating a fact. He had no doubt that Carolyn wouldn't hesitate to wake up the entire Colorado banking community to get what she wanted.

"If you can't get the money, explain it to the kidnapper. Ask for more time."

"And if he refuses?"

"He won't."

She turned away from him and wandered around the table, checking out the equipment. When she came to the screen with the map and the red dots, she pointed. "What's this?"

"A map."

"I can tell it's a map," she said with some exasperation. "And not a very good one. If you want more detailed maps of the area, we've got plenty. Dylan uses them to keep track of the different fields, pastures and grazing rotation."

He hauled himself out of the comfortable chair and went to stand beside her. The top of her head came up to his chin. In her boots, she was close to six feet. A tall woman. He liked that.

He pointed to the red markings. "These dots represent incidents of sabotage."

She counted. "Seven incidents. Since my brother hasn't seen fit to keep me informed, can you tell me about them?"

Burke had plenty of details. During the interrogations, he'd listened to dozens of complaints from ticked-off cowboys. "Like you said before, it was just petty mischief until the barn burned down."

Her soft pink lips frowned. "I still don't understand why. We're good neighbors. We provide employment to the people in this area. Why would anybody do this to us?"

"You want motives?" He flipped open the notepad where Silverman had recorded their notes. "There are over twenty names listed. People who bear grudges against the Carlisles."

She leaned over the table. Her manicured fingernail—a feminine contrast to her ranch clothes—skimmed down the list. "I don't even know half these people. How did you come up with this list?"

"Your employees told us about them. By the way, all the ranch hands were quick to say that they like their jobs and your brother is a good, fair-minded boss."

She pointed to a name on the list. "Who's this?"

When he bent down to see where she was pointing, her ponytail brushed against his cheek. The scent of lilacs from her hair distracted him and it took a moment for him to read the name. "He works for an oil company. Your brother wouldn't allow his equipment access through Carlisle property."

"That hardly seems like an incitement to vandalism. Or kidnapping."

Though Burke agreed, he knew better than to overlook any motive, no matter how slight. Some people could work themselves into a homicidal frenzy over a stubbed toe.

She read another name. "Nate Miller. That's no surprise. He's hated us forever, blames us for his father's failure on the Circle M."

"There are a couple of other ranchers on the list who don't like the competition from Carlisle Ranch."

"It's business," she said. "Why make it personal?"

"Your success hurts their bottom line. People tend to take bankruptcy personally."

"But we're always fair. Always." She tapped the name with her finger. "Dutch Crenshaw runs the meatpacking plant in Delta. We've given him millions of dollars in business over the years."

Burke considered Crenshaw's motive to be one of the best. "But you're thinking about building your own slaughterhouse."

"I gave him a chance," she said. "I told him that we wanted to use state-of-the-art humane technology, but he refused to modify his plant."

"So you're going to put him out of business."

She frowned. "Okay, maybe you've got a point."

His focus on the list was interrupted by a loud crash, followed by the sound of gunfire. The shots came from the front of the house.

Chapter Five

Burke's risk assessment had been dead wrong. They were under attack. He caught hold of Carolyn's upper arm and turned her toward him. "Go upstairs. Don't turn on any lights and—"

"The hell I will." She wrenched free. "Those were gunshots. Somebody's firing at my house—the house that's been in my family for three generations, the house my grandpa built. Don't ask me to hide behind the lace curtains in my bedroom."

Stubborn woman. "I go first. Stay behind me."

"Of course. I'm not going to put myself or anyone else in danger."

He grabbed his handgun from the shoulder holster slung across the back of a chair, aware of seconds ticking away. Whoever fired that shot would be making his escape. Moving quickly through the house, Burke turned off lights as he went. Carolyn followed in his footsteps.

Her brother staggered into the moonlit hallway, rubbing his eyes. "Carolyn? What's going on?"

"Stay with him," Burke ordered as he flipped the latch on the front door. "I'll be right back."

Leaving Carolyn behind—thank God—he slipped outside onto the veranda. Aware that he might be the next target for a man with a rifle and a nightscope, Burke stayed low. He dodged around the rocking chair and porch swing. At the end of the veranda, he jumped over the railing and ducked into the shadows.

Wind rustled the bare branches of a cottonwood. Nothing else appeared to be moving.

"Over here, Burke."

Burke followed the sound of the voice and saw a security guard crouched behind a truck that was parked on the wide gravel space beyond a hitching rail. Burke hustled toward him. "Where's the shooter?"

"Didn't see him. I was behind the house when I heard the shots."

His heavy jaw was thrust forward. His name, Burke remembered, was Neville. He'd been in the Secret Service for five years before joining Long-bridge Security. "What about a vehicle?"

Neville shook his head. "I didn't hear a car."

Cautiously, they peered around the truck. The driveway leading to the house was a long gravel lane. The yard was about an acre of winter-brown grass, separated from the road by a whitewashed fence. On the other side of the road, the land turned rugged with lots of trees and rocks—plenty of hiding places for a sniper.

"He could be dug in behind those rocks," Burke said.

He nodded. "A decent rifle would be accurate from four, maybe even five hundred yards away."

After that first burst of gunfire, no other shots had been fired. Likely, the shooter had already high-tailed it out of there. "Do you think he's gone?"

"I don't want to test that theory by taking a bullet," Neville said.

"Let's find him," Burke said. "You go right. I'll go left. We'll meet at the fence by the road."

As Burke moved across the yard, he scanned the cold, moonlit landscape. There was virtually no cover. Burke longed for the city streets, crowded with parked cars and doorways to duck into. This sniper was probably an expert hunter. Not like the city punks who held their guns sideways, more concerned with looking cool than taking careful aim.

When he reached the fence and no other shots had been fired, he was fairly sure that their sniper was gone. He heard the door to the house open. A mob spilled onto the veranda. Carolyn and her brother were both carrying rifles. The other three FBI agents accompanied them.

Lucas and two other cowboys—also armed—

charged toward the veranda from the two-story bunkhouse.

"There are way too many guns on this ranch," Burke said. This was the land of the Second Amendment where the right to bear arms would not be infringed upon. He turned and looked across the road. From where he stood, he spotted four good positions for a sniper to hide, if he'd even bothered to take cover. With Neville behind the house and no one else keeping watch, the sniper could have stopped in the road, dropped to one knee, taken aim and fired. But why? What did he hope to gain by rousing the household?

"Sorry I missed him," Neville said.

"Not your fault. One man can't patrol an area this size."

As he and Neville walked up the drive toward the house, Burke shivered in the December cold. He wasn't wearing a jacket or hat, and hadn't bothered to put on gloves. Responding to the threat had been his sole focus.

The gunfire bothered him because it didn't make sense. As a rule, kidnappers kept close tabs on their hostages.

But two men had abducted Nicole. One could be with her while the other came here. Why? By now the kidnappers had to know that the FBI had been called in. Why take the risk of coming close?

He stopped behind the black rental van he and

his men had driven from the Delta airfield. The back window was shot out, and there was a neat bullet hole in the rear license plate. None of the other vehicles showed signs of damage. The FBI van had been the target.

Carolyn stepped up beside him. Her rifle rested on her shoulder. "Looks like a pretty clear message, Burke. Somebody doesn't like you."

For a moment he grinned. He liked a challenge.

AFTER SHE'D HERDED EVERYONE back into the house, Carolyn took Burke and her brother into the office to talk strategy.

Somehow Carolyn had to turn the situation around and make it work. *But what can I do?* She couldn't put in extra hours to get the job done. It didn't matter that she was smart and strong. She couldn't change fate.

Pacing on the carpet, she snapped at her brother, "Don't drink that coffee. Caffeine keeps you awake."

"Somebody needs to be alert." He leaned against the desk and faced the sofa where Burke sat. "Looks like we made a mistake."

"What's that?" she asked.

"The kidnappers don't want the FBI involved."

"Of course they don't." Her temper flared. "That's exactly why Burke and his men are staying here. We need their expertise."

"Why? We're paying the ransom. I'm not taking any chances with my wife's safety."

"You want reasons?" In spite of her brother's distress, she had to be brutally honest. "I don't think I can get my hands on a million dollars in cash by the deadline."

"Why not? I'm sure there's a way."

"Even if we pay, there's no guarantee that the kidnappers will bring Nicole back."

A muscle in his jaw twitched. "I know."

"We're ranchers, Dylan. We don't know squat about crime. The best way to deal with these kidnappers is to follow the advice of experts. Right, Burke?"

He didn't bother to nod. Instead, he sat in self-contained silence. She couldn't tell what he was thinking, but hoped he had some kind of plan that involved more than sitting here waiting for the next call from the kidnappers.

Lucas Mann poked his head into the office. "I got a question for you, Carolyn. The men are asking if maybe you could see fit to give their guns back."

"Seems to me that you've got plenty of other guns."

"Well, sure." He raked his fingers through his thinning salt-and-pepper hair. "Most everybody has backup weapons. But we want all the firepower we can get. Especially since some polecat is shooting at us."

"And I suppose you're missing your pretty new Glock nine millimeter?"

"Ain't she a beaut?" A proud smile stretched his face, and she noticed the wad of chewing tobacco that made a pouch in his cheek. "I bought it when all this sabotage started up. Gave my old piece to MacKenzie, that new kid."

"I'm assuming," Burke said from the sofa, "that you legally transferred ownership."

"Speaking of sabotage," Carolyn said, quickly changing the subject. If Burke got official about the paperwork for all the firearms on this ranch, there would be trouble. "What's your opinion, Lucas? Who do you think is behind it?"

"Don't know who," he said, "and I don't know why. But it all started when we moved a couple hundred head onto the south grazing pasture, near the Widow Grant's property."

Dylan grumbled, "Don't start."

"Carolyn asked a legitimate question," Lucas said. "And she deserves an answer."

Apparently, there had been a dispute between these two. "Please, Lucas, continue."

"The first time I found a fence post torn down, I told Dylan that we should herd them cattle to a different area. He wouldn't hear a word of it. Then we had another incident. And another. Dylan still wouldn't change his mind. He sure can be pig-headed. Not meaning any disrespect."

"I didn't move the cattle," Dylan explained, "because I'm trying a new system of rotating the herd."

On the sofa, Burke leaned forward. His heels hit the floor with a loud thump—a subtle but effective way to get their attention. "Lucas, can you tell me why having cattle in that pasture might provoke vandalism?"

"Don't know why. I just wanted to keep the herd safe."

"They weren't in danger," Dylan said.

"We were damn lucky we didn't lose any cattle when they broke through the fence."

"Stop bickering." Carolyn felt her temperature rising. "I don't give a damn about what happened yesterday or last week. We need to concentrate on now. Right now. This very minute."

Lucas took a backward step, hoping to escape. She caught him with a glare. "How do you explain this, Lucas? When you put those cattle in a pasture that's usually empty, our men would be paying more attention to that area. Right?"

He thought for a moment. "Yep."

"So, these vandals would be more likely to get caught when the cattle were there."

"Guess so," Lucas said.

She spread her hands, palms up, presenting them with her conclusion. "It's counterintuitive to attack there. Why would they take the extra risk?"

"Because they're not very smart," Dylan said.

Clever enough to burn down the stable without being caught. She turned away from her brother before she snapped his head off. "Lucas, tell me about the fire."

"It was late." He shifted the tobacco wad to his other cheek. "And damned cold. Everybody was in bed, but I couldn't sleep and I remembered Polly had left some peach pies. So I came back here to the house for a midnight snack. That's when I saw the flames."

"You raised the alarm?"

"Yep."

"I'm sure the sheriff investigated. Did he say how the fire was started?"

"Nothing fancy. That stable was dried-out wood. All it took was gasoline and a match."

Burke unfolded himself from the sofa and stood. His height made him an impressive presence. "I have a plan."

Her automatic reaction was to object, but Carolyn was desperate to make some kind of forward progress, even if it meant stepping back and letting Burke take charge. "I'm listening."

"If we were in the city right now, I'd call in every free cop and state patrolman to provide surveillance and protection on the ranch."

"We ain't in the city," Lucas pointed out.

"But we have resources. A lot of men and a lot of guns."

She watched as her brother turned his attention toward Burke. Their gazes locked. They seemed to be communicating at a level she couldn't comprehend. Man to man.

Dylan gave a slow nod. "I think I know what you're planning."

"We need to set up a perimeter around the ranch," Burke said. "Deploy men at every place the security could be breached."

"All around the ranch?" She hated this idea.

"The house, the barn, the bunkhouse, all the nearby structures. The center of activity."

"You make it sound like we're under siege."

"Maybe we are."

"I like it," Dylan said. He set down his coffee, pushed away from the desk and took a step toward Burke. For the first time since Nicole's kidnapping, he grinned. "The next time these guys get close, we'll catch them."

Though the two men didn't bump chests and exchange high fives, she felt the testosterone level in the room raise by several degrees. Deploying armed cowboys sounded like a shortcut on the road to disaster.

Chapter Six

The next morning after she showered and dressed, Carolyn went downstairs to the kitchen where Polly had four burners and a grill fired up. With the efficiency of a short-order cook, she assembled breakfast burritos and wrapped them in foil. "Good morning, Carolyn. Hungry?"

"All I want is coffee."

Though she was trying hard not to show her agitation, her insides churned like a washing machine. She couldn't stop thinking about the sabotage, the list of enemies and the million things she needed to do today. Most of all, she was concerned about Nicole.

"How are you holding up?" Polly asked.

"I'm worried." Carolyn filled a mug from the coffee urn. "I've been meaning to tell you that I'm sorry I missed Thanksgiving."

"It was quite a feast," Polly said. "I even made that oyster dressing that Nicole likes so much. I don't think anybody else took a bite of it."

"Cowboys don't eat sushi. Or anything that resembles it." She sipped her mug, amazed that Polly could make gallons of coffee in an urn taste like custom brew. "How's Juan doing?"

"My husband is full of energy this morning. He walked down to the bunkhouse. Using his cane, of course." She paused her whirlwind of activity to pat Carolyn on the cheek. "We've all got to keep up our strength. Now, what can I get you to eat?"

Her stomach was far too tense to consider food. "Just coffee for now. But I'll be back."

Taking her mug, she went down the hall to the office, looking for Dylan or Burke. Instead, she found Lucas, Neville and the new kid, MacKenzie. They'd set up a whiteboard with some kind of schedule. One of Dylan's detailed topographical maps was spread on the coffee table with chess pieces scattered across it.

MacKenzie jabbered into a walkie-talkie. His language was vaguely military, using terms like "Roger that" and "Bravo team" and "Boots on the ground."

"What's this?" she asked as she pointed to the whiteboard.

"A surveillance schedule," Lucas explained. "We set up a perimeter. All these chess pieces on the map are different guys. Neville used to be in the Secret Service. He showed us how to maximize our security."

Neville, the Longbridge security guard, gave a sheepish shrug. "As you can see on the hour-by-hour schedule, I've worked in downtime so the men can rest, but nobody wants to take a break."

"Cowboys aren't always good at following orders," Carolyn said. "Too damned independent."

"So I've learned," Neville said.

Lucas chuckled. "I'll tell you what, there ain't going to be nobody taking potshots at this ranch house."

Which still didn't put them any closer to finding Nicole. She turned to MacKenzie. With his brown hair flopping over his forehead and freckles across his nose, he looked about twelve years old. "Where did you get the walkie-talkie?"

"I found them," Lucas said. "Remember a few years back, before everybody got cell phones, we tried using these things. Didn't work too good."

She remembered. Several of the walkie-talkies got lost or thrown away, mostly because the men didn't like having somebody check up on them. Consensus among the ranch hands had been that the old ways of communication were the best. Everybody had cell phones now, which were mostly kept turned off unless a cowboy on the range wanted to make a date with his honey in Riverdale.

MacKenzie obviously enjoyed this opportunity to play G.I. Joe. He turned away from her and spoke into his walkie-talkie. "Listen up, y'all. HQ is awake and on the move."

Amused, Carolyn asked, "What does that mean? HQ?"

"We gave everybody nicknames," MacKenzie said. "You know, like the real Secret Service. When they talk about the President, they call him POTUS. It stands for President Of The United States."

"I thought HQ would mean headquarters. Is it a person?"

"Yes, ma'am. It's you."

She glanced over at Lucas and Neville who appeared to be doing their best not to laugh. "What does that stand for? HQ?"

"That's not important." MacKenzie looked a bit scared. "We had to come up with a whole lot of code names really fast. Like your brother. He's BB for Big Boss. And Burke is TF for Tall Fed."

"And HQ?"

"Ma'am, it stands for Heifer Queen. And that's not saying you're a cow or a heifer, which is a cow that hasn't had a calf. It means you're the queen of the whole ranch, cattle and all. And that's accurate because you're—"

"Stop." She held up a hand to forestall further excuses. "My code name from now on is…Carolyn."

"Yes, ma'am."

She pivoted and left the office. Heifer Queen. It wasn't the worst thing she'd been called.

BURKE CHECKED HIS WRISTWATCH. Approximately one hour and ten minutes ago, the first gray light of dawn had crept across the windowsills in the dining room. He'd pulled up the shades and given tasks to his three agents. Dylan had joined them.

After they had coffee and something to eat, Corelli, dressed in his suit and tie, had cleared away the plates. Agent Corelli was a bit obsessive-compulsive—an appropriate character disorder for someone who worked with complex and often frustrating electronics.

Now, they had settled into a routine of monitoring phone calls, studying maps and pacing. Waiting.

Burke looked toward the door to the dining room, anticipating the moment when Carolyn would appear. In addition to the pleasure of seeing her, he needed her help to execute a plan that might bring her sister-in-law home safely. Only Carolyn could help him; she held the key.

When she finally came through the door with coffee mug in hand and her smooth black hair falling loose to her shoulders, her gaze went straight to him. Without speaking, she seemed to be asking a question. Without threatening, she threw down a challenge.

How the hell would he convince her to do something she most likely wouldn't want to do? Sweet talk wouldn't work; she'd see right through him.

Nor could he scare her into going along with his plan because this woman was fearless. Burke figured his best tactic was honesty.

Dylan slung his arm around her shoulder. "About time you got up, sis. It's almost half past eight."

She hugged him back. With their long lean bodies, matching black hair and green eyes, they looked like a male and female reflection of each other. The yin and yang of the Carlisles.

"Anything happening?" she asked. "Other than a bunch of crazy cowpokes yakking on walkie-talkies and pretending to be surveillance experts?"

"Don't be snippy," Dylan said. "Setting up the perimeter gave the men something to do. It's not like anybody can concentrate on work while this is going on."

Burke noticed that neither brother nor sister had mentioned Nicole's name. They held the anguish he knew they must be feeling at a distance, and he appreciated their tough, taciturn attitude. In other kidnapping cases he'd worked, the families had been devastated to the point of breakdown. This was better.

"Good morning, Carolyn," he said, remembering to be polite. "Deploying the ranch hands might look crazy, but you've got to admit that we're well protected. Nobody's going to get close enough to take another shot at this ranch."

"I'm sorry about your van," she said.

"It was a rental."

Dylan directed her to a computer monitor where Agent Corelli sat with headphones. "Let me show you the setup. All of the landlines for the phones are routed through this monitoring station. The ringers are turned off, which is real good. Everybody we know has been trying to get in touch with us. Those calls are going straight to voice mail."

"How will the kidnapper get through?"

"If the number he used last night comes up, Corelli will let it ring. He does the same with any call that isn't from a familiar number."

Burke circled the dining room table and stood beside her. "Dylan and I practiced how to handle a call from the kidnappers. The same way I showed you last night. I think your brother should take the next call."

"I want to hear his damn voice," Dylan said.

She lifted her chin and studied her brother for a long moment. She approved of what she saw, and nodded. "Fine with me. In about a half hour, I need to get busy talking to the bankers about that million-dollar ransom."

Burke stood close enough to smell the lilac fragrance of her shampoo. He needed to get her alone to make his pitch. "Before you get started with the finances," he said, "I want you to take me to the field where all the sabotage started."

"Shouldn't you be here at the house? If the kidnappers call, Dylan might need your expertise."

"Agent Silverman is a trained negotiator. And Dylan knows how to handle himself." Burke checked his wristwatch again. Managing time gave him the illusion that he was in control, even though he knew that the only agenda that really mattered was dictated by the kidnappers. "If we leave now, we can get back by the time the banks open."

"I suppose I could take you over to the south pasture. Actually, I wouldn't mind getting outside."

Dylan dug into his pocket, took out a set of keys and held them out. "Use my truck. It's parked in front."

"Burke, you can drive," Carolyn said as she pulled her cell phone from her pocket. "That way I'll have my hands free to get started with my phone calls."

They made their way past the two cowboy bodyguards with their walkie-talkies and rifles on the porch, and then drove to the front gate where they encountered two more cowboy guards. Both of them tipped their hats to Carolyn.

"Take a right, Burke." She cast a rueful gaze at the guards. "With all these guns and the surveillance, it feels like we're conducting some kind of military operation. Baghdad in Colorado."

He appreciated the protection, even if it was excessive. But that wasn't what he wanted to discuss with her.

Burke needed to get inside the SOF compound and take a look around. Using force was out of the question. Survivalist groups were notoriously volatile, and he didn't want to provide an armed standoff. Carolyn had a natural inroad. She could use her influence with Sam Logan to set up a meeting. Unfortunately, from what she'd said yesterday, he didn't think she'd be too keen on talking to her former boyfriend.

The two-lane road curved around a thick stand of pines. When they came around the trees, the view took his breath away. Snowcapped peaks reached into a cloudless sky of pure blue. Forested foothills bordered a terrain of brownish grass and shrubs. The leveled, cultivated earth beside the barbed wire fence was surprisingly verdant with long rows of two to three inch shoots. "Green? In December?"

"Winter wheat," Carolyn said.

When Burke was growing up with his single mother in Chicago, he'd spent several summers in Wisconsin dairy-farming country with his grandparents. They were schoolteachers and lived in town, but he'd spent enough time with local kids to learn the basics of riding horses and life on a farm. "I've never seen the winter wheat."

"Soon enough this crop will go dormant when we get more snow, but I love the way it looks right now. The green promises new life. And hope."

They were approaching the herd. Across an open space, he saw the boxy black silhouettes of Angus cattle. He'd been told there were only a couple of hundred head on this pasture. *Only?* It looked like a lot of cattle to him. The magnitude of this sprawling ranch operation impressed the hell out of him. "How far does your property extend?"

"Far enough," she said. "Slow down. Here's where we turn."

He made a right onto an unpaved gravel road. The truck tires bounced over a cattle guard. At the metal fence, Carolyn hopped out to unlatch the gate for the truck to drive through and closed it behind them. Though she was bundled up in a black shearling coat and wearing a flat-brimmed hat, he'd never confuse her with a cowboy. Her gait was purely female.

She climbed back into the truck. Her eyes were bright. "Thanks for bringing me out here, Burke. I needed to smell the land, to hear the cattle lowing. Music to my ears."

"Another golden oldie?"

"How about 'Moo-oo-oon River?'"

"Very funny," he said. "There's another reason I wanted to get you alone. I need your help, Carolyn."

"Hold that thought," she said. "We've got another gate to go through."

As she repeated the opening and closing procedure on the second gate, he reconsidered his plan. He had no right to ask her to get involved with Logan and the SOF. She wasn't a trained investigator, and he might be leading her into danger.

Instead of getting back into the truck, she motioned for him to drive forward and get out. "Come with me, Burke."

She strolled through the field toward the herd.

In Wisconsin, he'd seen plenty of cows, but those were friendly black-and-white-spotted Holsteins. These heavy-shouldered Black Angus looked rugged and undomesticated. Beef cattle. Western cattle.

Her cell phone rang, and while she answered, he stroked the solid flank of a steer that turned, glared and ambled toward a water trough. The south pasture wasn't open range. A barbed wire fence ran from the road to the rugged cliffs of the foothills. He noticed a trail outside the fence.

Carolyn finished her call and joined him. "That was my attorney. He's not happy about paying a ransom."

"Neither am I," he admitted.

"There might not be a choice."

Her tone was crisp and matter-of-fact, as if she were discussing a business transaction instead of a kidnapping. He wondered how long her strict self-control would last. How much pressure could she take?

As she casually smoothed the hide of another massive steer, she asked, "Why are we here?"

"I wanted to see the field where the sabotage took place so I could figure out why it happened here."

"Easy access," she suggested. "It's close to the road."

"But still hidden from direct sight of the ranch house." He pointed to the trail at the edge of the fence. "Where does that lead?"

"They call it the Indian Trail. It connects with a pass through the mountains." She tipped back the brim of her hat and looked up at him. "You said you needed my help."

He nodded. "You know who I consider my number one suspect."

"Sam Logan and the SOF." The moment she spoke his name her expression darkened. "You could be right. From what Polly said, it sounds like those guys like to cause trouble."

"I want to get inside the SOF compound and take a look around."

"Go for it, Burke. Do you need a search warrant?"

"It's going to take more than a piece of paper. A militia group that's opposed to government interference isn't likely to open their gates to a fed. This could end in a standoff."

"Like Waco," she said.

"It occurred to me that Logan might be convinced to show off for his old girlfriend. He might even offer to take you on a tour."

Her eyes narrowed. "You want me to call Logan and ask him if I can come inside?"

"We need to get in there."

"I can't do that." She lowered her head and stalked back toward the truck. Halfway there, she turned. "Logan hates me. What makes you think he'd respond to me?"

"Ego," he said. "Logan is the head of the SOF. He'll want to brag, to show you how important he is."

"Damn it, you could be right." She circled the truck and climbed into the passenger seat.

As soon as Burke slid behind the wheel, she started talking again. "Even if I could convince him to let me into his little kingdom, I don't see what good it will do. Logan might be a jerk, but he isn't stupid. If he's involved in the kidnapping, he won't lead us to Nicole. Not unless I have a million bucks in my back pocket."

"You can try."

Her cell phone rang again. She answered in a brisk tone, then inhaled a gasp. "How did you get this number?"

She looked at him with terror in her eyes.

"What is it?" he asked.

"Please hold on," she said into the phone. "I can't hear you. Let me put you on speakerphone."

Pressing a button, she held the phone so he could hear.

"Go ahead," Carolyn said.

"This is the kidnapper," said a scratchy falsetto voice. "I bet you're glad to hear from me."

What the hell? In his years of negotiating, Burke had never encountered a second introduction call. Last night, they'd heard his demands. Was this a second kidnapper?

The voice continued, "Do what I say and Nicole won't get hurt."

Chapter Seven

The last thing Carolyn expected was a call from the kidnapper. Corelli had all the equipment for this call set up at the house, and this squeaky voice was nothing like the whisper from last night. "Who is this?"

"Nicole is wearing a plaid shirt, red and blue. Wrangler jeans. The inside of her wedding ring says *My horizon*."

Carolyn felt the blood drain from her face. Very few people knew about the inscription on the wedding rings. "Is Nicole there? Let me talk to her."

"I want five hundred thousand in cash. By Monday night."

"Half a million?" Why had the amount dropped? Why was the deadline changed?

"You'll pay."

"Yes," she said quickly. "Don't hurt her. Please don't hurt her."

"I'll call again, Carolyn."

The phone went dead.

What just happened? Staring through the windshield, her vision blurred. It felt like she was going to pass out.

Gently, Burke took the phone from her hand. Her arm fell limp to the seat. All the strength left her body as she collapsed against the seat on the passenger side of the truck.

"Carolyn." Burke sounded like he was a million miles away instead of sitting beside her. "Carolyn, look at me."

She was too devastated to move, couldn't even summon the will to turn her head. She mumbled, "I did all the wrong things. Didn't ask for proof of life. Didn't keep him on the phone. I messed up."

Burke flipped back the center partition and pulled her across the seat toward him. Weak as a rag doll, she rested against him. The warmth of his body did little to melt the chill she felt inside. As if her heart had frozen. *Why is this happening to my family? Why?*

A sob tore from her lips. She fought desperately for control. *I'm not the kind of woman who cries.* She forced herself to hold back the storm of emotion that had been building inside her. Her hands clenched into fists and she held them against her mouth, pressing hard.

"It's okay." Burke stroked her trembling shoulders. "Let it out."

Still she fought. If she turned all weepy, nobody would respect her. Hell, she wouldn't respect herself.

"Go ahead and cry," he whispered. "I won't tell a soul."

Another sob wrenched through her. Another agonizing gasp. Her body convulsed. The floodgates burst. Tears poured down her cheeks. She completely lost control. For a long moment, she clung to him, weeping and trembling.

"It wasn't the same guy," she said between sobs. "Not the same as last night."

"Probably not." He caressed her hair. "It wasn't the same voice or phone number."

"But he knew about the wedding ring." Her tears streamed. "How could he know?"

"There were two men who abducted Nicole." His calm, rational voice soothed her. "Maybe they had a falling out. Maybe they went their separate ways."

"Why?"

"That's what we need to find out."

"You're right." And her outburst was wasting precious minutes. Ashamed and scared and angry, she pushed against his chest, separating herself from him. "What should we do?"

He held up his cell phone. "I'm calling Corelli. If that phone number from the call is listed, he can give us a name."

Still shuddering from the outpouring of emotion,

she sank back against the seat and listened to Burke's end of the conversation. While he talked, he linked his hand with hers.

From the moment they met, he'd told her that he didn't come to Carlisle Ranch to make friends. He'd warned her that some of his advice would seem cold and hard. But she'd felt his compassion. With her free hand, she pulled her shirt collar out of her jacket and dabbed the moisture from her cheeks. It had been years since anyone saw her weep. Even when her father died, she'd kept her tears to herself.

Ending his call, he squeezed her hand. "Are you okay?"

"I blubbered all over you, and I don't even know your first name. What does the J.D. stand for?"

"Jeremiah Davenport."

She could understand why he went by initials. "You're definitely not a Jerry."

"Or a Davenport," he said. "Let's get back to business. Who would call you on that phone? Who has that number?"

"This is my personal phone," she said. "It's not the PDA I use for business. Some people in Denver have this number, but very few. That's why I used this phone to contact my financial people. I wanted to keep the line clear."

"Here at the ranch," he said, "who knows the number?"

"Only Dylan." *But somehow the kidnapper knew.*

"Last night when we heard the gunshots, where was your phone?"

She cast back into recent memory. "I was in the dining room, talking to you. The phone was in my hand. I set it down on the table."

"And when we responded to the gunfire?"

"I left my phone on the table. Didn't pick it up until much later."

"After half the people on the ranch had come into the house. Any of them could have picked it up and gotten your private number."

She didn't like the direction this conversation was taking, but she couldn't deny his logic. "Are you saying that someone on the ranch is working with the kidnappers?"

Burke's cell phone jingled and he answered.

Dark thoughts of betrayal flooded her mind. When she'd learned of the many people who held grudges against the Carlisles, she'd been surprised and hurt. This was worse. Someone who worked for them—a trusted employee—was involved in Nicole's kidnapping. Anger sparked inside her, burning away the last vestige of her tears. When she got her hands on that traitor, they would pay dearly.

"We're in luck," Burke said. "The kidnapper's call came from a public telephone in Riverton."

FIFTEEN MINUTES LATER, Burke parked the truck at the only gas station in Riverton—a small town that was about ten miles from Delta and an equal distance from the Carlisle Ranch. He'd considered taking Carolyn back to the safety of the ranch house but decided it was more important to follow this lead as quickly as possible.

The public phone hung on a dingy brick wall beside the closed doors of the auto repair bays. The windows of the gas station were dark. "What time do they open?"

"Whenever Silas O'Toole gets around to it. Usually, that's from about ten in the morning until six at night."

When the kidnapper called Carolyn at a few minutes after nine, he had a reasonable expectation of privacy. Using the public phone was actually a clever move because their trace resulted in a dead end.

It seemed unlikely they'd find any witnesses in this dusty little western town. Main Street's sidewalk stretched one block with storefronts and offices on either side. Limp red bows hung from the streetlights in a feeble attempt at Christmas decorating. At the other end of the block was a bar with a Closed sign hung on the door. The only activity appeared to be at Winnie's Café where two vehicles were parked outside at the curb.

Burke had already put in a call to Sheriff Trainer in Delta, requesting a forensic team to take finger-prints from the phone. Not that he expected to find much in the way of evidence. Even amateur criminals knew enough to wear gloves.

"I don't see many pedestrians," he said.

"Most of the people who live here work in Delta. Even the kids are bussed to school." She cracked her door open. "Shouldn't we be poking around and asking questions? Someone might have seen the kidnapper using the phone."

"I hate to have you involved in this." Any kind of investigation carried a certain element of danger. And he was concerned about her emotional state.

"You need me," she said. "People around here don't like to talk to strangers, especially not to a big city guy in a leather jacket who's carrying an FBI badge."

"But they'll talk to you."

"They'd better."

Her smile showed a cool determination that he hardly believed was possible after her torrential breakdown. In the space of fifteen minutes, Carolyn had not only recovered her poise, but actually seemed stronger.

Though there was something to be said for Western stoicism, he'd seen the passion that burned inside her. Reaching toward her, he wiped away a smudge the tears had left on her cheek. "You're okay?"

"A hundred and ten percent." Her long black lashes fluttered as she blinked. "I won't fall apart again. My dad always used to say, 'When you get thrown from your horse, the best thing is to get right back on.'"

He didn't see how that advice applied. "What's that mean?"

"Don't waste time sitting on your butt and crying."

She climbed out of the truck and he followed. He unzipped his leather jacket, allowing easy access to his shoulder holster.

They talked to two women on the street, an insurance agent and the owner of the feed store that was directly across the street from the gas station. Everybody was friendly to Carolyn, but none of them had seen anyone using the phone.

Their next stop was Winnie's Café. The front window was painted with a Santa Claus and a snowman. As soon as they stepped through the door, he heard Carolyn curse under her breath. She nodded toward a wiry man in a beat-up Stetson. Like the hat, his face was weathered. Leathery brown skin stretched tight across high cheekbones and a sharp chin. Burke guessed that he was probably near forty.

Quietly, Carolyn said, "That's Nate Miller."

He remembered the name from the list of potential kidnappers. Miller blamed the Carlisles for the loss of his cattle ranching business. He had leased his property to the Sons of Freedom. "Introduce me."

He could see her jaw tighten as she approached the square wood table where Nate sat reading the sports page of the Denver newspaper and sipping coffee.

Keeping her voice level, Carolyn greeted him. "Mind if we join you?"

"Suit yourself." He squinted at Burke through hostile eyes. "I haven't seen you around here before. Has this got something to do with what happened to Nicole?"

Though he obviously knew about the kidnapping, Nate hadn't offered condolences or any expression of concern to Carolyn. That was cold. "What time did you get to the café this morning?"

"Same as every damn morning. Nine o'clock."

That gave him enough time to stop at the gas station and make the ransom call. "Did you drive?"

"Must have." He sneered. "That's my truck sitting outside at the curb."

Carolyn's cell phone rang. She carefully checked the number before she said, "Excuse me, gentlemen. I need to take this call."

As she politely stepped away from the table, Burke watched for a reaction from the man who sat opposite him. Nate Miller didn't move a muscle, didn't betray any sign of his grudge. When he lifted his coffee mug to his lips, his hand was steady.

If Miller was one of the kidnappers, he had to be the coolest criminal Burke had ever encountered, and that list included professional hit men, bank robbers and terrorists.

"Do you live in town?" Burke asked.

"I've got a little place up the road near Delta. It belonged to my ma before she died."

Nicole could be there. "Address?"

"I don't have to tell you."

Burke slid his FBI shield from his pocket and placed it on the table. "Yeah, you do."

"FBI." He sneered. "Of course, the high-and-mighty Carlisles would call in the feds. They know people. They've got more money than is right."

"You know what happened to Nicole."

"I heard about it. Everybody's buzzing." He set his mug down on the table. "It's a shame. Nicole's a nice woman. Can't say the same for her husband."

"Somebody might have kidnapped her to get back at him."

Anger flared in his squinty eyes. "It's no secret that I hate the Carlisles. Because of them, I lost my livestock and my livelihood. My wife left me. Took my son. If it wasn't for Sam Logan paying me big bucks to rent my land, I'd have lost my ranch, as well."

When he stood, Burke growled, "Sit down, Miller. I have more questions."

"Here's your answer." Miller remained standing. "I didn't kidnap Nicole."

Burke had no intention of letting this guy walk

away. He glanced around the café. There were only four other customers. Burke saw no reason to bust up this pleasant little establishment if this confrontation turned physical.

He took out his wallet, peeled off a twenty, dropped it on the table and stood. "Let's take this outside."

Miller made a beeline for the door and Burke followed.

Still on the phone, Carolyn watched with concern in her eyes. He gave her a wink. If it came down to a fight, he could take Miller without breaking a sweat. Not only was Burke six inches taller and probably forty pounds heavier, but he knew how to fight. He'd been taught by the best at Quantico. Before the FBI, he'd had five years on the street as a Chicago cop.

Truth be told, he almost wanted Miller to resist. Carolyn had eased her tension with tears. Burke would find a similar release in kicking butt.

On the sidewalk, Miller turned to face him. His thumbs hitched in his pockets. Not a fighting stance.

"Here's my address." He rattled off a street number. "Is that all you want from me?"

"Where were you last night?"

"Home in bed. Alone."

"Before that?"

"I work as a handyman now that I don't have a

ranch to take care of. And I had a light day. I was done by two."

"Can anyone verify your whereabouts?"

His thin mouth curved in a smirk. "I own a horse. You could talk to him."

Burke had faced men like Miller before. Men who believed they'd been wronged and the world was against them. They expected the worst. And they lived their mean little lives for the sake of their grudges. Even if Miller had nothing to do with Nicole's kidnapping, he was taking great pleasure from the pain this caused Dylan and Carolyn.

"This morning," Burke said, "when you drove into town on your way to the café, did you pass the gas station?"

He gave a nod. "I did."

"Did you see anyone?"

"Matter of fact, I did. I noticed because I needed a fill-up, and I thought O'Toole might have opened early. But it was just a guy using the phone."

"Did you recognize him?"

"Sure. It was Sam Logan."

Chapter Eight

Burke and Carolyn, who continued talking into her cell phone, returned to the gas station—which still wasn't open for business. Sheriff Trainer had parked beside the Carlisle truck, and Trainer himself leaned against the wall beside the phone. When he saw them coming, he stubbed out his cigarette and tossed the butt in a trash can.

"Is this the phone?" the sheriff asked.

Burke nodded. "Be sure to check the coins inside for prints."

"You got it. Anything else?"

"Do you know Nate Miller?"

"He's a mean son of a gun. When his wife separated from him, she had to take out a restraining order. I guess they patched things up since then because she withdrew the order and, from what I understand, she lets him visit with his kid."

"I want you to search his house."

The sheriff showed very little surprise. "You think he kidnapped Nicole?"

"He's a suspect." And a man without an alibi. "He claims he was alone all day yesterday. Difficult to verify, but see if you can find anyone who saw him. After that, I'd appreciate if you could come out to the ranch house."

"I'll be there." He reached inside his jacket pocket and took out a toothpick wrapped in cellophane, which he peeled. He stuck the pick in the corner of his mouth. "I sure wish I'd done things different. The first time Dylan called me about the sabotage, I should have undertaken a serious investigation, maybe even called in the state cops."

"Do you think the kidnappers are the same guys?"

"Don't you?"

"The obvious conclusion isn't always correct." As an investigator, Burke kept an open mind to all the possibilities. "This investigation is going to be a whole lot easier when our eyewitness can make an ID."

"The security guard," Trainer said. "How's he doing?"

"Still unconscious. The doctors expect him to wake up, but they won't say when." He returned to more positive action. "I want a detailed, thorough search at Miller's house. Copy the hard drive of his computer. Search his files. Check for footprints and fingerprints. If there's a single hair from Nicole's head, I want you to find it."

Trainer bit down hard on his toothpick. "We've got the forensic equipment and the training. But I can't guarantee that we won't miss something. We're not as experienced as the Colorado Bureau of Investigation."

Burke didn't want to involve another law enforcement agency. Last night he'd arranged for other FBI investigation teams—a chopper and tracker dogs. All of whom would answer directly to him. "I'll send Agent Smith over to Miller's place to give you a hand. See you back at the ranch."

In the truck, Burke held off on telling Carolyn about Miller's supposed sighting of Logan at the public phone. Nate Miller was an unreliable witness. And she appeared to have her hands full with bank negotiations. Since the moment she'd answered that call in Winnie's Café, her cell had been glued to her ear.

His suspicions turned toward the inside man at the ranch. Someone—one of those supposedly loyal cowboys—had taken her phone and passed the number to the kidnappers. Burke considered gathering up all the cell phones and running a check on recent numbers called. But that still wasn't proof. The inside man could have used somebody else's phone. It was better not to alert the traitor that they were looking for him.

Carolyn disconnected her call, sank back against the seat and exhaled in a long whoosh. "I've got the ransom."

"How's it going to work?"

"With reams of paperwork, transfers of funds and a friendly contact at the Federal Reserve Bank. One million in cash."

"I'm impressed." Truly he was. Not many people could summon up a million in cash on a few hours' notice.

"In our business, we regularly handle large transactions," she said. "In addition to our own herd, we work with sixty other cattle ranches of various sizes."

He remembered her earlier explanation of their international business. "Other producers of certified organic beef. They're contracted with you for distribution."

"We pay them on delivery of their stock, even when we don't have payment from the end purchaser."

She took off her hat and smoothed her black hair into a ponytail. Though she looked like a cowgirl, she'd gone into high-power executive mode. She was an impressive CEO, no doubt about it.

And yet, she'd wept in his arms. Normally, he didn't respond well to tears, but he'd been relieved when Carolyn had her outburst. Even when vulnerable, she was strong. The only woman he had ever loved had been formidable—a law professor—tough, independent and intelligent. Sexy as hell.

Much like Carolyn.

"My attorney," she said, "is working through our Denver bank to get the cash. He'll charter a helicopter and deliver the ransom after lunch."

"A million dollars is going to make a heavy package."

"I've thought of that," she said. "The money will be placed in one of those giant mountain-climber backpacks."

"Sounds like you've handled every detail." Though she didn't look like the strain had affected her, he purposely lightened the mood. "Here's what I think. We should take that backpack and hike to the top of a fourteener. We unzip the pack and we throw all that cash into the wind."

She gave him a puzzled look. "Why?"

"Greed is a prime motivator in crime. From kids stealing hundred-dollar sneakers to million-dollar ransoms, it's all about greed. Get rid of the money and you'll cut down on crime."

"For a fed, you have some strange ideas."

"Haven't you ever thought of what it would be like to live on a deserted island without a penny to your name? Surviving on coconuts and berries."

"My fantasies run more toward riding off into the sunset and never looking back." Finally, she grinned. "Just ride forever. No more spreadsheets, stock quotes, negotiations and conferences. A simple life."

He'd like to give her that peace of mind. He wanted to see how she acted when she wasn't under life-and-death stress. Would she laugh when he made jokes? What was her favorite food? More importantly…what was she like in bed? Though he had no right to think about her that way, his imagination formed an immediate picture of Carolyn stretched out naked on satin sheets, her black hair fanned out on the pillows, her arms reaching for him and her toes pointed.

He shook his head to erase that vision. After this ordeal, she'd never want to see him again. His mere presence would be a reminder of this terrible chapter in her family history.

"We need a plan," he said.

"For what?"

Her full lips parted. Her eyes were warm and expectant, as if waiting for a kiss. Instinctively, he leaned closer to her. His voice lowered. "A plan for when we get back to the ranch. If the kidnapper has an inside man, we need to be sure he doesn't overhear any of our strategy. For example, we don't want him to know you've arranged for the ransom."

"I get it."

"Good." He was pleased with himself for reining in his fantasies and sounding rational.

"But I need to tell Dylan. He needs to know about the inside man. And the ransom." Her fleeting grin was replaced with renewed tension. "You're right about throwing the money away. If we weren't rich, Nicole would never have been kidnapped."

"True." Kidnapping was a crime that affected the privileged. "But if you were poor, you'd have a whole different set of problems."

Her lips were pinched. "As soon as we get to the ranch house, I'll tell Dylan we have to talk in private. I'll take him upstairs to my bedroom. You meet us there."

AS THEY ENTERED THE RANCH house, they put their plan into effect. While Burke briefed his men and dispatched Agent Smith to assist the sheriff with his forensic investigation at Miller's house, Carolyn pulled her brother aside.

Grabbing a mug of black coffee, Burke headed upstairs to join Carolyn and her brother. He climbed halfway up the polished wood staircase and looked down. A husky cowboy whose name he didn't recall sauntered through the front door. The newly hired MacKenzie bounded past him, talking nonstop into his walkie-talkie. From the kitchen, he heard Polly giving instructions to her cooking crew who grumbled back at her. Too many people had access to the ranch house; finding the traitor wouldn't be easy.

He continued up the staircase. The dark green carpet runner muffled the thud of his boot heels. On the landing he hesitated. He and his men were housed in guest rooms at the north end of the upstairs hallway. Carolyn had told him that her bedroom was the second door on the south. Without knocking, he stepped inside.

A tall glass cabinet beside the window housed a display of riding trophies and blue ribbons, but that was the only hint of cowgirl. Her furniture was modern with clean lines. Blond wood and burgundy. Her bed was neatly made.

In different circumstances, entering her bedroom might have been akin to entering the Promised Land. Not now. The tension in this room was thick.

Carolyn stood by the window, scowling fiercely. Dylan's hands were clenched into fists. He looked like he was ready to punch a hole in the smooth, cream-colored wall. Apparently, Carolyn had already given him the bad news.

"I can't believe it." His jaw was so tight that his lips barely moved. "A traitor. One of my own men."

"I'm sorry," Burke said. And he meant it.

"There is good news," Carolyn said. "I've made all the arrangements for the money. It'll be delivered by three o'clock."

"Dylan," Burke snapped his name, compelling his attention. "The information about the ransom is the kind of thing we need to keep secret. When the kidnapper calls again and you talk to him, don't tell him you have the cash. Ask for more time."

"Why?"

The truth was brutal, but it was better to face reality. "As long as he doesn't have the ransom, he needs to keep Nicole alive. She's his bargaining chip. And we need proof that she's all right. Do you hear me?"

Dark circles surrounded Dylan's eyes. In their depths, Burke saw a terrible pain. He'd experienced that agony. He knew the hell of losing someone you loved, and he knew there was nothing he could say or do to alleviate the suffering.

Dylan squared his shoulders. "Until the kidnapper calls, what do we do?"

"We investigate. As we speak, the sheriff is executing a search warrant on Nate Miller's house."

A commotion from downstairs interrupted him. It sounded like twenty cowboys on horseback had stormed through the front door.

The three of them hustled from the bedroom to the staircase. A redheaded cowboy waved from the bottom of the staircase and held up a manila envelope. "I found it. Here it is. I found it."

Burke reached down and plucked the sealed envelope from his hand. In square block letters, it read: "Dylan Carlisle. Proof."

"Where did you find this?" Burke asked.

"Tied to a fence post in the south pasture." A huge grin split his face. "I went to feed the herd and there it was. I didn't open it. On account of it was addressed to Dylan."

Dylan patted his shoulder. "You did the right thing."

Actually, Burke would have preferred having the envelope left in place. There might have been clues, like footprints or the way the knots were tied. "Agent Silverman is going to open the envelope. He'll need to handle it carefully in case there are fingerprints or DNA."

In the dining room, they stood waiting while Silverman—wearing latex gloves—slit the edge of the envelope and removed a photograph.

"A Polaroid," Silverman said. "You don't see many of these anymore. Not with digital cameras."

The picture showed Nicole with a determined smile on her face. She held the front section of today's newspaper.

"Proof of life," Carolyn whispered.

Silverman placed the photo on the table. "Don't touch it. I doubt we'll find fingerprints, but we might get lucky."

As the others crowded around to take a closer look at the photo, Burke moved to the end of the table where Corelli was still monitoring phone calls. In a low voice, he issued instructions. "That's a Denver newspaper. Find the delivery time in this area, the locations for delivery and a list of local subscribers. Get the sheriff to canvass stores where the paper is sold."

"Got it." Corelli gave a nod.

"Is there any way to set up continual surveillance on that south pasture? It's about thirty acres."

"I could do it with satellite," he said. "I don't have that kind of equipment here, but I could interface with Denver. Don't get your hopes up, Burke. The mountains are hard to search. It depends on sight lines and location."

Burke grabbed the red-haired cowboy who was still beaming proudly. "I need for you to think carefully."

"Sure thing."

"Describe the terrain in the area where you found the envelope."

"It was up by the trees. I wouldn't have noticed at all except for this." He reached into his pocket and pulled out a long yellow scarf. "I saw it flapping in the wind."

"It's Nicole's." Dylan took the scarf from him and gently caressed the material. "I bought it for her myself."

Technically, the scarf was evidence and needed to be treated as such. But Burke doubted there would be any viable prints or DNA after being stuffed in the cowboy's pocket. There was no harm in allowing Dylan to cling to this scrap.

Turning away, he glanced at Corelli. "How about surveillance in the south pasture?"

"The best surveillance for this much land is probably a helicopter."

"I've already arranged for a chopper." He'd made that call last night. His superior had objected to the expense, but he reminded them that the FBI was investigating this kidnapping at the request of the governor.

He checked his wristwatch. "They should be here by noon. They're also bringing tracking dogs."

Corelli raised an eyebrow. "Things are about to get real exciting around here."

"Is there anything else you can do with computers? What about thermal imaging?"

"I brought a heat-sensing camera with me. It's long range. I can scan from about fifty yards away."

"That might come in handy."

Carolyn appeared at his side. "Come with me."

She led him through the front door and into the yard. When they were out of earshot of the cowboy guard posted on the porch, she whispered, "Nicole was giving us a clue."

"Enlighten me."

"Her hands. The way she was holding the newspaper." She illustrated. "On one side, she held it with her thumb and forefinger. On the other, she had three fingers outstretched."

He studied her hands for a moment. "A circle on one side. And the letter *M* on the other."

The Circle M Ranch, headquarters for the Sons of Freedom, was the clue.

"It's time," Carolyn said tersely. "We need to pay Sam Logan a visit."

Chapter Nine

Carolyn knew how to control her emotions. Since childhood, she'd been trained to keep her outbursts to herself. *Never cry. Never shout. Don't even laugh too loud.*

But the rage she felt as she took the turnoff leading to the Circle M surged too close to the surface. Her pulse raced like a stampede. If Sam Logan had done this terrible thing, if he'd snatched Nicole, she'd kill that bastard with her bare hands.

She pulled onto the shoulder and parked.

"What's wrong?" Burke asked.

"I need to get a grip." Fiery embers exploded behind her eyelids. She could barely see straight. "I'm fighting mad."

He removed his sunglasses. "Look at me, Carolyn."

As if that would do any good. Burke wasn't the most calming presence in the world. "Leave me alone. I'll manage."

But he cupped her chin and turned her face toward him. She had no choice but to stare into his dark eyes. His gaze held her. In the morning sunlight, his irises were a rich, chestnut brown. His features seemed set in granite.

"How do you do it?" she asked. "In your job, you deal with bad guys all the time. How do you keep from lashing out?"

"Do you hunt?"

"Only with a camera."

A smile twitched his lips. "You grew up on a ranch and you don't hunt?"

"I don't like killing animals. What's your point?"

"My hunting analogy was supposed to make you think of focus. Emotion comes from your right brain. The left brain is logical. If you start thinking with logic, planning what move you're going to make next, you'll pull some of the focus away from your anger."

"Planning," she said. "I'm good at planning."

"Think about what you're going to say to Logan." His voice was calm. "Concentrate on what steps we need to take. Once we're inside the SOF compound, we need to assess the area. Make a mental map of the buildings. If they're holding Nicole, where is she? Who would know where she is? Somebody must be bringing her food and water. Which person is most likely to help us?"

"Think of the end goal."

"We need names," he said. "Usually, I can count on Corelli to pull up this kind of information, but the SOF is too insignificant to be on the FBI radar. If we have individual names, we can run them through our database."

"I'm good at remembering names."

"Me, too." He caressed her chin. "You're trembling."

"Holding back my anger." She needed an immediate release—a way to express the raging emotion that rushed through her veins.

"How can I help?"

Without thinking of the consequences, she slid out from behind the steering wheel and across the bench seat of the truck. She moved into his arms, pressing against him.

They kissed, hard and fierce. She willingly surrendered to her passion. Her body arched toward him. The pressure of his mouth against hers sparked a fire within her. It felt good. A controlled burn. Like the kind the forest rangers set to stop a wider conflagration.

Her lips parted. She drew his tongue into her mouth. Her senses went wild. Every cell in her body responded to him.

When he separated from her, she was breathing in gasps. She hadn't cooled down. In fact, the opposite. But this fire made her stronger, braver, better. She felt like she could take on the world.

One creepy ex-boyfriend like Sam Logan was no problem.

She turned the key in the ignition and drove to the gate outside the Circle M. Between sturdy gate-posts, a double-wide gate—about five feet tall with horizontal white slats—was latched and locked with a chain. A dusty-looking cowboy ambled toward them, rifle in hand.

Carolyn parked at the side of the road, hopped down from the truck and strode toward him. "Tell Sam Logan that Carolyn Carlisle has come calling."

"Don't care," he said defiantly. "Nobody gets in. No trespassing."

"Use your cell phone." She wasn't about to let some half-baked guard stand in her way. "Tell Logan I'm here."

Burke had gotten out of the truck and stood behind her. The cowboy glanced toward him, then back to her. "I'll call."

She and Burke stepped back. His kiss still burned on her lips, and she was incredibly attuned to his presence. If they'd been alone, she would have been all over this tall, handsome fed, but that wasn't an option. She was here to gather information from the SOF, to find Nicole.

She leaned against the hood of the truck and watched as the cowboy returned to his guard position and took out his cell phone. Burke stood beside her.

"Logan will be out here in a minute," she said. "You were right about his ego. He won't be able to resist bragging about how he's the big shot leader of a gang of crazies."

"After he shows, what's your plan?"

"I'll get him to invite us in."

Though she kept her focus on logic, she couldn't think of a single rational reason why Logan should open his doors to her. Her method of persuasion had to be based on emotion. She'd mention their past relationship. "Have you ever been in love, Burke?"

"Have you?"

"You're doing that negotiator thing," she said. "Answering my question with a question of your own."

"Yes, I've been in love. It changed my life." Through his sunglasses, he looked at her. "And you?"

"Not with Logan. When we were together, it seemed like the right time to get married and settle down on the ranch. But I didn't love him."

"How did he feel about you?"

"It might have been love." She'd had years to analyze this failed relationship. "Or he might have been in love with the idea of getting a piece of Carlisle Ranch. My father liked him. If we'd married, Logan would be a rich man today."

"Maybe," Burke said, "he was using you."

A rueful awareness seeped into her thoughts.

Years ago, when she broke up with Logan, he'd seemed shattered. He'd tried everything to win her back. "You think he was only after my money?"

"It fits the profile for a cult leader—someone who's manipulative, egotistical and uncaring about the needs of others. With SOF as his power base, Logan has found a way to use these people and, apparently, to provide himself with an income."

"All these years," she said. "I've felt guilty for rejecting him."

"Which is how he wanted you to feel."

The road on the opposite side of the gate led to a barn. A stand of trees blocked the view of the house and the other outbuildings. Logan rode toward them on that road. A majestic sight on his pure white horse. His dark brown leather vest looked like a doublet. He was bareheaded, and his long blond hair flowed past his shoulders and glistened in the sunlight.

At the gate, he reined his horse and looked down at her. In the six years since she'd seen him, she'd forgotten how truly good-looking he was. Not as tall as Burke, but broad-shouldered and lean. His features were as picture-perfect as a movie star's. No wonder she'd fallen for him.

Carolyn ambled toward the gate. She climbed the slats to the top rung, making her nearly as tall as Logan on horseback. She looked directly into his baby blue eyes. "Well? Aren't you going to invite me inside?"

"You look good, Carolyn. City life agrees with you."

Instead of giving him the satisfaction of telling him that he was still as gorgeous as ever, she patted his horse's neck. "This is a fine-looking stallion."

"I'm keeping him for stud."

"Is that what you do here?" She bit the inside of her cheek to keep from smirking. "Stud service?"

"We train horses. One of my men is Butch Thurgood, a rodeo champion bronc rider."

She'd never heard of Thurgood, but Carolyn didn't keep up with the latest rodeo news. "I'd like to meet him."

"I remember when you used to be the queen of the barrel race." He glanced toward the guard with the rifle. "Back in the day, me and Carolyn were a couple. I considered marrying this young woman, joining with her to become part of the all-powerful Carlisle family. Imagine that. Me, being a corporate, capitalist stooge?" He gave a completely phony laugh. "I came to my senses and saw the error in my ways."

Spare me the sermon. "Last night, when my brother and the sheriff came by, your men wouldn't allow them to enter."

"We don't recognize the law represented by Sheriff Trainer." He looked past her to Burke. "Or by your friend over there. FBI?"

"Special Agent J. D. Burke." He took a step

forward. "I haven't come here to accuse you, Logan."

"I don't believe you."

"I don't have a search warrant or a judge's order," Burke said. "Carolyn and I are merely looking for information. We want to talk to your people. To find out if anyone saw anything suspicious last night when Nicole Carlisle was kidnapped."

Logan sneered. "The government and the agents of the government are liars."

"I'm not armed." Burke held his coat open, showing his empty shoulder holster. Apparently, he'd left his handgun in the truck. "I just want to ask questions."

"We're neighbors," Carolyn said. "Aren't neighbors supposed to help each other in times of need?"

"Carlisle Ranch represents the establishment. You and your brother are the nemesis of freedom."

She tamped down her anger. It wouldn't do any good to insult him. "You knew my father, Logan. He liked you, believed in you."

"Sterling Carlisle was a good man."

"I'm not your enemy." *Not yet, anyway.* "Please let me come inside. I'm worried about Nicole. Maybe one of your people saw something. Maybe they can help me find her."

He dismounted, passed the reins to the guard and unlocked the gate. With a sweeping gesture, he announced, "I have nothing to hide."

Entering the Circle M, she strode down the road, flanked by Logan and Burke.

In her younger days, she'd been satisfied in a relationship with a handsome cowboy like Logan. Now, she needed more complexity, more depth and a hundred times more honesty—qualities Burke had in abundance.

In a conversational tone, Burke asked, "How many people live here at the Circle M?"

"Gathering information for your FBI database?"

"We keep track of groups like yours," Burke admitted. "But I'll tell you the truth, Logan. We don't have a listing for Sons of Freedom. You're not dangerous enough to be on the radar."

"Just because you haven't heard of me," Logan said, "doesn't mean I'm not important."

"The FBI has bigger fish to fry. Terrorists. Hijackers. The Russian Mafia. Those are the real enemies of the state."

Logan puffed out his chest, possibly hoping to inflate his bruised ego. "You have no idea who you're talking to."

"How many people have you got here? Ten or fifteen?"

"Twice that. Twelve men and fifteen women and children."

"Husbands and wives?" Burke asked.

"We don't believe in the overregulated institution of marriage."

"How does that work?" Carolyn asked.

"If a couple chooses to be monogamous, their decision is respected. If not, that's accepted."

"Are you monogamous?"

"Not at present." His blue-eyed gaze slid over her body. "Sorry, Carolyn. You already missed your chance to be with me."

Silently, she thanked her lucky stars.

Burke asked, "How much acreage do you have?"

"Enough to live on. Nate Miller is trying to sell the rest of his land. Hasn't had much luck."

"And how do you pay the bills?"

"The Sons of Freedom are establishing a new way of life, based on the real foundations of America. Self-sufficiency, simplicity and old-fashioned hard work." He glanced toward Carolyn. "I'm writing a book."

The World According to Peabrain? "I didn't know you could write."

"A man can do anything he sets his mind to."

They were within sight of the main buildings. Compared to the Carlisle ranch house, the Circle M was plain and shabby. The house was a simple, one-story structure with beat-up siding the color of soured milk and a shingled roof in need of repair. The other outbuildings were equally ugly. A shiny, new double-wide mobile home was parked near the ramshackle barn.

She saw two women walking together. Each of

the women's hair was pulled back in a bun. Beneath their jackets, shapeless dresses hung to their ankles.

"Interesting fashion statement," she said. "You say that a man can do anything. What about a woman?"

"Our women are respected and revered," he said. "They're the glue that holds civilization together. They raise our children, provide sustenance and create a healthful environment."

To Carolyn's ears, his language was code for cooking, cleaning and popping out babies. "That doesn't sound like much of a life."

"Not to someone like you." His upper lip curled in a sneer. "A career woman."

What did I ever see in this jerk? His golden hair, broad shoulders and perfect features didn't make up for his ridiculous, misogynistic ideas. "You haven't changed a bit."

"Because I've always been right." His sneer turned into a dazzling white smile. "Our women are happy here. You'll have plenty of opportunity to talk to them and hear for yourself."

"Wonderful." The way she figured, some of these respected, revered ladies had to be dissatisfied. They were probably the best lead to finding Nicole.

Two cowboys stalked toward them. Unlike their leader, they weren't smiling.

Logan motioned to the taller of the two and issued an order. "Escort Carolyn to the kitchen. She can help the ladies prepare lunch."

She hadn't come here to peel potatoes. "If you don't mind, I'd rather—"

"I do mind," Logan said. "We have a division of labor. The men discuss business. And the ladies…"

"Prepare lunch?"

"I'm glad you understand. Run along now."

Nobody, but nobody, told her to run along. She was the CEO of an international corporation. She negotiated with heads of state. She knew the governor.

But this wasn't about her. She was here to get information about Nicole. And the women would probably be more sympathetic than the men.

Baring her teeth in a false smile, she said, "You boys have a good time. Don't tire yourself out with too much heavy thinking."

She pivoted and strode toward the ranch house.

Chapter Ten

Burke watched as Carolyn stormed toward the house. The cowboy who accompanied her tried to take her arm and she yanked away so fast that he stepped back, giving her plenty of space. *Smart move.* After Logan's women-belong-in-the-kitchen comments, Carolyn was volatile.

Though she could probably take care of herself, Burke still didn't like the idea of being separated from her. When entering a dangerous situation, partners should stick together.

"I see the way you're looking at her," Logan said.

"I'm concerned," Burke said. "She's a victim. A kidnapping hurts the family almost as much as it hurts the person who has been abducted."

"Carolyn's a fine looking woman."

Burke lied, "She's not my type. She'd just as soon kick my ass as kiss me."

The short cowboy who stood with them chuckled. Burke introduced himself and got the other man's name—Wesley Tindall. If he got enough names for Corelli to investigate through criminal databases, they might have a clue about what actually went on at the Circle M.

He looked toward the bunkhouse where two guys were working on a huge piece of machinery. "Installing a generator?"

"I told you. We want to be self-sufficient. Except for the house, all our heat comes from propane."

"But you still have to buy the propane tanks."

"We have a big stockpile."

Burke cringed inside. If it came to a showdown with the SOF, a stray bullet could penetrate the stockpile of propane tanks and cause an explosion that would rock the mountains. "Let's get down to business, Logan. I'd like to interview your men. Someone might have noticed something unusual last night."

"Like what?"

Logan's voice sounded suspicious. The best way to get information from this guy was to constantly feed his giant ego. "Damned if I know. This case has me baffled. You might have some ideas."

The handsome blond cowboy shrugged. "Ask your questions."

"First, I'd like to get my bearings." Burke took a couple of steps and looked beyond the bunkhouse to the west. "I'm a city guy. Pretty much lost in all this wide-open space."

"I've lived here all my life," Logan said smugly. "I know every rock and tree."

Burke deliberately pointed in the wrong direction. "Is the Carlisle Ranch that way?"

"Not even close." Logan aimed his forefinger like a gun. "The house is over there—only about four miles away as the crow flies. Following roads, it's more than that."

"And where's the Widow Grant's place?"

"Do you see that break in the hills? It's an old Indian trail. Widow Grant lives just south of there."

Carolyn had mentioned the Indian Trail at the edge of the south pasture where all the sabotage had taken place. Burke wondered if it was significant.

Logan asked, "Why are you interested?"

"Nicole was kidnapped by two men on horseback somewhere between the Widow Grant's place and the Carlisle ranch house. Do you think the kidnappers came this way? Toward the Circle M?"

"Our land is fenced with barbed wire. Nobody came through here on horseback."

"Why is it fenced? You're not running cattle."

"Horses," Logan said. "We keep them in the barn at night and let them run free during the day."

Looking toward the barn, Burke noticed a surveillance camera attached above the door. Another lens was visible on the mobile home. No attempt had been made to hide the cameras. "You have electronic surveillance."

"State-of-the-art, equipped with night vision," Logan drawled. "Some people don't like us. We need to keep ourselves protected."

Were the fences and the surveillance used to keep people out? Or to keep the Sons of Freedom in? "Any chance that I could take a look at the footage from last night? The cameras might have picked up something that would help me find Nicole."

Logan showed no sign of being worried. "What time was she kidnapped?"

"Before dark. Somewhere between five and six o'clock."

"You're out of luck," Logan said. "During the day, we have enough people around to make sure nobody breaks in. We generally don't turn on the surveillance until after dinner. That's around seven or eight. Too late to show anything that would be useful to you."

He'd answered quickly, almost as if he knew the time of Nicole's kidnapping before Burke had told him. Was she here? In addition to the mobile home, the house, two bunkhouses and the barn, there were several smaller buildings. Storage sheds. A smoke-house. Other motor homes and trailers. There was probably a root cellar under the house.

Altogether, there were too many damn places for Logan to hide a kidnap victim…if she was still alive.

IN THE RANCH HOUSE KITCHEN, Carolyn was the only woman wearing jeans and boots. Her clothing wasn't the only thing that made her different. She stood taller. She had energy, fire and ambition.

These three women—dressed in shapeless frocks, limp sweaters and leggings—seemed like the life had been drained from them. After they politely introduced themselves using only their first names, they returned to their chores, quietly performing their tasks with dedication and zero enthusiasm. Like prisoners, they seemed robbed of their will, caught in an endless cycle of boredom. What could possibly cause these young women to come to this place? Why did they stay?

"I hear you raise horses," Carolyn said. "This would be a wonderful afternoon for a ride."

"The men handle the horses," said the tall blonde who appeared to be in charge of the kitchen. Her name was Sharon, and Carolyn guessed they were the same age—mid-thirties. The other women were at least a decade younger.

"We get to brush and curry the horses," peeped a very pregnant woman who had identified herself as Sunny. She waddled across the kitchen floor with all the grace of a Mack Truck. Her formerly blond hair had grown out several inches at the roots.

"Do the men let you muck out the stables?" Carolyn asked.

"Sometimes."

"Lucky you." Carolyn laughed into a pall of silence.

There was about as much vitality in this group as a gathering of tree slugs. Somehow, she needed to get them talking, to find out if they'd seen or heard anything that might lead to Nicole.

Sauntering across the gray tiled kitchen floor, she zeroed in on Lisa—a scrawny brunette with tattoos of thorns around both wrists. "You seem familiar," Carolyn said. "Are you from around here?"

"No, ma'am." She concentrated on chopping a zucchini into one-inch cubes. "I grew up in Denver."

"That's where I live most of the time. Maybe we met there," Carolyn said. Remembering Burke's suggestion that they get names that could be run through the FBI database, she asked, "What's your last name?"

Sharon cleared her throat. "When we joined the SOF, we gave up our last names. This is a new life. A fresh start."

Sunny teased, "Lisa wants her last name to be Richter. She wants to be Mrs. Pete Richter."

"No, I don't." The paring knife in Lisa's hand trembled. "I don't like Pete. Not that way."

"You don't have to pretend anymore. Not since your sister took off." Sunny explained to Carolyn, "Both Lisa and her sister had a thing for Pete."

"But your sister left?" Carolyn questioned.

"Yes." Lisa centered another zucchini on the chopping block.

"Do you know where she went?"

A single tear slid down Lisa's cheek. "She's gone."

"Forget about her," Sharon said harshly. "Your sister was a fool. She wasn't suited to our lifestyle."

Carolyn rested her elbows on the counter beside Lisa and spoke quietly. "I've lost someone, too. My sister-in-law, Nicole. Yesterday, she was knocked unconscious and kidnapped. I'm trying to—"

"I know who you are," Sharon said. "Carolyn Carlisle of the fancy-pants Carlisle Ranch. You own half the county. Why should we help you?"

"Because it's the decent thing to do. Like it or not, we're your neighbors. We need your help."

In her business, Carolyn was accustomed to tense negotiations with international distributors and local ranchers. These three women were the most hostile group she'd ever encountered.

"Let me tell you about Nicole," Carolyn said. "She's a good and decent person. She's worked all her life as a large-animal veterinarian. The first time I met her, she'd spent the night in the stall with a horse that had colic. She was exhausted, barely able to walk. But she was grinning because the horse recovered. A good person."

"We don't care," Sharon said.

Carolyn continued, "Nicole married my brother five years ago. They're deeply in love, trying to have a baby." She went to stand beside Sunny. "It's hard for Nicole to get pregnant. She's had internal injuries."

Sunny frowned. "That's too bad."

"When are you due?"

"In a couple of weeks, I think."

"You're seeing a doctor, aren't you? Or a midwife?"

Sharon stepped between them, positioning herself as a shield and precluding any further conversation. This tall blonde, who would have been stunning with makeup, looked Carolyn in the eye. "You should leave. Now."

Her pupils were dilated, and she licked the corner of her mouth. Was she on drugs? Carolyn said, "Logan wanted me to help you with lunch preparations."

"Fine," Sharon said. "Then you need an apron."

"Right." *I need an apron like I need a toe growing out of my forehead.*

THE INTERIOR of Logan's double-wide mobile home was an office with fairly high-end equipment. Apparently, the SOF goal to live like pioneers didn't preclude the use of computers, scanners and GPS mapping instruments.

Burke operated under the assumption that Logan's

survivalist philosophy was a convenient cover story for some other endeavor. Probably criminal and lucrative. If Corelli could hack into these computers, they could decipher the real basis for the SOF in about five minutes.

Under Logan's supervision, he'd spoken to ten different men, most of whom were typical taciturn cowboys. The notable exception was a guy with a thick Brooklyn accent who admitted that the only cowboys he'd seen before moving to Colorado were in the movies.

"That's everybody," Logan said. He sat behind his big oak desk with his chair tilted back and his boots propped up on top. "Like I told you, nobody saw anything out of the ordinary."

"You said there were twelve men." Though Burke hadn't taken notes, he'd memorized every name. "I counted only ten. And I didn't meet that rodeo star you mentioned. Butch Thurgood?"

Logan's gaze sharpened. He didn't like being caught in a lie. "Butch and Pete are in Denver for a couple of days."

"And what about the ladies? I'd like to talk to them, too."

"The women keep busy. They didn't see anything."

"Never can tell," Burke said. "Sometimes, women notice more details than men."

Logan stuck out his lower lip. Petulant, like a child. "I don't encourage gossiping and nosiness."

Or independent thinking? For the life of him, Burke couldn't figure out what Carolyn had ever seen in this petty tyrant. Sure, Logan was handsome, but so was a tiger before it ripped your arm out of the socket.

Logan continued, "The women who live here are grateful to have a roof over their heads. Some of them came from the streets. SOF is a fresh start for them, and they're happy to be obedient and hard-working."

Burke sensed an undercurrent to this speech. Was there dissatisfaction among the ladies? A rebellion brewing? If he wanted to find out what was really going on inside the SOF, he needed to listen to the women. Maybe Carolyn was having some luck in talking to them.

He rose from the straight-back chair beside the desk. He'd already affixed one bug under the lip of Logan's desk, but he had another listening device that he wanted to get inside the house. "Let's pick up Carolyn at the house, and you can show us around."

"Nothing special to see."

"Looks like you've added a lot of improvements."

"Nothing special," Logan repeated.

"What about a meeting place?" He was hoping for

a big room with slogans on the wall or other trace-able clues. "It's like you're running a little town here."

"That's right," he drawled. "And I'm the mayor."

"Where do the kids go to school? Where do you all sit down to eat?" *Where's your stash of propane tanks? Where would you hide a kidnapping victim?*

"We meet where we eat in the men's bunkhouse. It's nothing fancy, just a big plain room with tables. There's a wall that separates the meeting area from the sleeping area."

"And a television?"

"Why would you think that? We're trying to lead a simple life here. Like the noble American pioneers who settled the West."

And wiped out the native population? Burke wasn't impressed with the phony rhetoric. "I assumed you had television because I saw a dish on top of the house."

"We're connected to the outside world. At times, it's necessary to know what's happening." He shrugged. "Maybe, we watch the occasional football game."

Finally, Burke found common ground. "I have a friend with a skybox at Invesco Field. If you come into Denver, I'd like to take you to a Bronco game."

"Yeah?" Logan grinned. "A big guy like you probably played football."

"I did."

"Me, too. Quarterback. If I'd been on a halfway decent team, I would have made all state."

From outside the office, he heard the whir of helicopter blades. The FBI search team must be arriving at the Carlisle Ranch.

The moment of friendly bonding over football vanished as Logan glanced up. "One of yours?"

"Probably. I requested assistance. Choppers and dogs."

"Don't expect to enter this property again."

"Come on, Logan. We were getting along so well."

"We shoot trespassers." He pulled his long legs down from the desktop and stood in one smooth move. "We're done here."

WEARING A PLAIN MUSLIN APRON with old stains across the midsection, Carolyn looked up at the sound of the approaching helicopter. She felt like running into the yard and waving her arms, screaming to be rescued from the doldrums of the Circle M kitchen. This had been the most frustrating half hour of her life—peeling potatoes and trying to get these women to talk.

Hoping to engage their sympathies, she'd told several stories about Nicole. The only one who responded was the pregnant woman, Sunny.

The other two women, Sharon and Lisa, became even more sullen. At one point, Lisa sat at the table with her hands folded neatly and stared, unmoving, for a solid thirty seconds. When Carolyn asked if she was okay, Sharon informed her that Lisa was praying. Drugged was more like it.

Carolyn set down her potato peeler on the countertop and wiped her hands on the hem of the apron, being careful not to touch the prior stains. "I'm finished."

"Me, too," Sunny said. "Gather up your peelings in that rubber tub and we'll take it all out to the compost heap. Is that okay, Sharon?"

The blond woman nodded. Slowly.

Outside the back door, Carolyn walked beside Sunny toward a fenced-off area that would be a vegetable garden in the springtime.

"You have to help me." Sunny paused for a moment and scribbled on a scrap of paper with a pencil stub. "Please."

"Yes, whatever you need."

"Don't let them see you talking to me. Keep smiling."

Carolyn tossed her head and smiled, trying her best to look utterly mindless. "What's up?"

"I've got to get out of here before my baby is born."

"They won't let you leave?" Carolyn asked.

"I know too much. Can't explain now." She dumped her peelings onto a stinking compost pile, stood up straight and rested her hand on her huge belly. "Lisa's sister didn't disappear. She didn't leave. They killed her."

Dear God, this place is a nightmare. "What about Nicole?"

"Sorry, I don't know anything about her." She glanced over her shoulder. "Here comes Logan. Pretend like you're shaking my hand."

Carolyn did as she asked. With a huge smile, Sunny whispered, "Meet me at midnight tonight."

Carolyn pocketed the scrap of paper Sunny had passed to her. "Always glad to help."

Chapter Eleven

The most dangerous aspect of any incursion into hostile territory was the exit strategy. As Burke watched Carolyn saunter toward him and Logan, he hoped she wouldn't do anything to provoke retaliation. They needed to get the hell away from the Circle M.

Through his sunglasses, he noted the positions taken by three of the men he'd met. All were scanning the skies for the chopper. All were armed, and these weren't the type of rifles used by casual sportsmen. The Sons of Freedom had broken out the automatic assault weapons and sniper rifles. Evidence of this brand of firepower combined with the stockpile of propane tanks made the SOF an extremely volatile enemy—a fact that didn't seem to concern Carolyn in the least.

Without breaking stride, she unfastened the strings of her apron and peeled it off. She slapped the fabric against Logan's chest. "Thanks for your hospitality."

"It's good for you to work in a kitchen for once." He signaled to one of his men, who responded quickly. "Escort our guests to the front gate."

Burke made an attempt to keep the tenuous line of communication open. "I appreciate your cooperation." He held out his hand for a friendly shake. "This is an impressive operation."

Logan turned his back and walked away. Over his shoulder, he said, "Get the hell out."

Carolyn called after him, "Hey, Sam."

It was the first time she'd used his given name, which Burke thought was an effective use of a negotiating tool. Carolyn was sharp. In one word, she'd reminded him of their prior relationship.

He faced them. "What is it, Carolyn?"

"There's no call to be rude. The pioneers had a tradition of Western hospitality. When someone offers the hand of friendship, it's not right to turn away."

With his men watching, he couldn't be churlish. He grasped Burke's hand. In a low voice, he said, "We're not friends."

Logan turned to Carolyn with hand extended. When she placed her hand in his, he pulled her close. "You hurt me once, honey. This time, it's my turn."

"Is that a threat?"

"Not if you stay out of my way."

As he and Carolyn walked up the road to the gate, Burke held his silence. Earlier he'd counseled

Carolyn about containing her outrage. Now he had to apply those same restrictions to himself. *It won't do any good to explode.* He was smarter than that, better than that.

But Logan's smarmy attitude ticked him off. That blond son of a bitch with the perfect features was nothing more than a cowboy con man, hiding behind phony rhetoric about the noble American pioneers.

When Burke slid into the passenger seat of the truck, he immediately opened the glove compartment and retrieved his gun. The weight of it felt good in his hand.

"Your ex-boyfriend is one of the coldest, most calculating liars I've ever met, and that's saying a lot. I've dealt with terrorists and serial killers. Sam Logan disgusts me more."

"More than a serial killer?" Carolyn started the truck.

"Logan isn't crazy. He knows the difference between right and wrong. And he consciously chooses wrong."

She wheeled around in a U-turn and drove away from the Circle M. "What happens next?"

"When we get back to the ranch house, all hell is going to be breaking loose." Burke holstered his gun. "I'll need to coordinate choppers and dogs and a half-baked patrol of cowboys with rifles. Not to mention keeping everything quiet so the traitor can't report our every move to Logan."

"You're sure that Logan is the kidnapper?"

"Not a hundred percent." Logan's alibi was the SOF. They could all stand in a circle and swear that they were all together at the time of the kidnapping. Which didn't necessarily mean they were lying. "I'm certain he's engaged in some kind of criminal activity. Maybe he's got a meth lab hidden in one of the outbuildings. Maybe he's doing some kind of smuggling."

"His men were carrying some pretty fancy weapons. He could be trafficking in guns."

"Could be." As Burke started his left brain thinking, his anger faded. "In any case, he's using the SOF as a cover for himself and his sorry gang of outlaws."

"And the women?"

"He never lets them get involved in business, right?"

"Right," she said.

"I doubt they know what's going on. The women and children are, basically, hostages. Logan is using them as a human shield. The FBI can't come after him with guns blazing while there's a danger to innocent women and children."

Though they were still a mile away from the Carlisle Ranch, she pulled over to the side of the road and parked. "I need to talk to you about the women. I got the impression that some of them might be on drugs."

"Logan told me that some of the women came from the street, which I assume means they were either hookers or runaways." The thought of Logan approaching some poor soul down on her luck and luring her to his ranch revved up Burke's temper again. "He said they were lucky to have a roof over their heads."

"Not lucky at all," Carolyn said. "One of them was murdered."

He hadn't expected this bombshell. "Murdered?"

"One of them talked to me. Her name is Sunny. Can't be more than twenty years old, and she's pregnant. She wants to get away from the Circle M." She dug into her jeans pocket and took out a scrap of paper. "She wants me to meet her at this location. Tonight. At midnight."

He read the scribbled words on the scrap. "West field. By the pines."

"She mentioned a name, Pete Richter. Maybe she was trying to tell me he's the killer."

He recognized the name. "Logan said that Richter and Thurgood weren't at the ranch. They could have taken Nicole somewhere else. Or they could be guarding her in one of those outbuildings."

"We need to get back in there," she said. "We need to search."

Easier said than done. Following the legal parameters for a search with a warrant was out of the question. And Logan would never give up without a fight.

The only way Burke could search for Nicole was to send in an assault team. And risk the lives of the women and children at the Circle M? Even if it meant rescuing Nicole, he couldn't put others in danger.

AS BURKE HAD EXPECTED, the pastoral setting of the Carlisle ranch house had erupted into chaos. Polly was trying to serve lunch. The ranch hands with their walkie-talkies were still patrolling. An FBI team with bloodhounds and cadaver dogs had arrived. And the chopper pilot stood waiting for instruction.

Burke's first order of business was to delegate. He put Agent Silverman in charge of coordinating these various operations.

Neville and the cowboy protection patrol would keep up their surveillance with one major difference: they had to move out of Dylan's office and into the bunkhouse. As soon as they left, grumbling with every step, the noise level in the house returned to something near normal.

While Silverman prepared to deploy the chopper and the dogs with grid maps of the area, Burke took Carolyn and her brother back to her bedroom sanctuary. In the relative quiet, he filled Dylan in on what they'd discovered at Logan's compound.

Dylan turned to his sister. "What did you ever see in that jerk?"

"You liked him," she reminded. "Both you and dad were ready to march me down the aisle to marry him."

"Because I didn't want to see you move to New York and turn into a corporate witch."

"Like Mom?"

He exhaled in a whoosh. "Let's not paw through that old garbage, okay?"

"Have you called her? Told her about Nicole?"

Burke stepped in before their conversation deteriorated into what appeared to be an old family argument. "Dylan, I want you to work with Silverman to coordinate the search efforts. The FBI teams need backup from your men who know the territory. You should make those assignments."

"Got it," he said.

"Keep in mind that we've got a traitor in our midst. Don't tell any of your men about obtaining the ransom or our suspicions about the Circle M."

"What about the ransom?" he asked. "That money is going to get here any minute. How are we going to pick it up and still keep it a secret?"

"I've got it covered," Burke said. "It's better that you don't know the details."

Identical pairs of green eyes stared at him in disbelief.

"A million dollars in cash," Carolyn said. "*Our cash*. We need to know."

Clearly, she had a point. Burke quickly explained, "The ransom is being flown to Delta. We already have two Longbridge Security guards at the hospital watching over the man who was shot, and I figured—"

"How is he doing?" Carolyn interrupted. "Jesse Longbridge? Is he conscious?"

"Not yet. Technically, he's not in a coma because he's responsive to external stimuli. But he's still not awake." Which was unfortunate on many levels. If Jesse woke up and could give them an identification, they'd at least know who they were looking for. He continued, "Those two guards are picking up the ransom and keeping an eye on it."

Carolyn and Dylan exchanged a glance. Both nodded.

"I trust Longbridge Security," Dylan said. He headed toward the bedroom door. With his hand on the knob, he paused. "I didn't mean to snap at you, Carolyn."

"Same here."

When the door closed behind him a hush descended.

The atmosphere in her bedroom, though quiet, was charged with suppressed emotion. She'd perched on the edge of the bed. Her hair was out of the ponytail, tumbling loose to her shoulders. She tilted her head back and stretched, arching her throat. "Dylan never forgave Mom for leaving the ranch. He couldn't see how stifled she was. The ranching life isn't for everybody."

"Is it for you?"

"I have the best of both worlds. In Denver, I'm Corporate Sally. Out here? Annie Oakley."

He sat beside her on the bed—a move he might regret. Developing a relationship with the victim's family in a hostage situation was nearly inevitable, but empathy didn't include the kind of passionate kiss they'd shared in the truck. He'd already gone too far with her.

When she looked up at him with those intriguing green eyes, his discipline and training ebbed. He wanted to make love to this woman. When she reached up to stroke his cheek, he caught her hand.

"We can't do this," he said. Yet he didn't release her hand.

"Which part of me scares you the most?" she asked. "The businesswoman or the rancher?"

"Well, let's see. The CEO might drive me to ruin. But Annie Oakley might fire a blast of buckshot into my ass." He raised her hand to his lips and kissed her fingertips. "I'm not scared, Carolyn. Are you?"

"Not a bit."

In any other situation, making love would be the next natural step. He was drawn to her. The magnetism was palpable, so strong that he began to sweat. He forced himself to stand, still holding her hand. "We have a lot to do."

He pulled her to her feet and into his embrace. Just one kiss, he told himself. One more kiss wouldn't hurt.

But she stepped back. "I don't like unfinished business, Burke. Once I start on a project, I close the deal."

"Meaning?"

"I want more from you than just one kiss."

And he'd be happy to deliver. *The whole enchilada, baby.* "I suggest we continue this negotiation at a later time."

"Suits me."

When she left the bedroom, he followed. He had about a hundred things to do, but his focus at that moment was simple. He couldn't take his eyes off her long legs and round bottom in her snug jeans. Denim had never looked so good.

AFTER CAROLYN REALIZED there was nothing useful she could do in the house, she stepped outside to take a breather. Her path led, predictably, to the corral outside the barn where she climbed onto the fence railing and gave a low whistle.

Elvis approached, swinging his hips. At the fence, he leaned his neck toward her, welcoming a hug.

Mindful that someone might be listening, she kept her voice low. "Here's my problem, Elvis. Burke is just about the sexiest man I've ever seen in my whole life. He makes me want to drag him into the hayloft and make love."

Elvis nodded.

"It's totally inappropriate."

Not to mention heartless. How could she be fantasizing about lovemaking while Nicole was being held captive and her brother was going through hell? A chill took root in her heart—a dark cold that had nothing to do with the December weather.

In the proof-of-life photo, Nicole appeared to be uninjured. Was she tied up? Chained? Were they holding her in a dark cell? "Oh God, Elvis. What am I going to do?"

He shook his head, and his black mane flopped over the white blaze on his forehead. Just like a real shrink, Elvis always turned the question back to her. Rightly so. The answers were usually within her.

But this time there was very little Carolyn could do. She'd arranged for the ransom to be delivered, and she'd made contact with Sunny, who might be the key to getting inside Logan's compound. Other than that, she was helpless.

And what am I going to do about Burke? Clearly, her attraction to him was a way of distracting her from terrible thoughts about the kidnapping. If fear was cold, the way she felt about Burke was a bonfire.

"It's not like I want a relationship," she confided to Elvis. Though she and Burke both worked in

Denver and could certainly see each other again, she didn't expect anything long term. They were both too demanding, too competitive.

All she really needed from Burke was an uncomplicated moment of passion. After that, they'd go their separate ways.

Lucas came toward her. "Hey, Carolyn. Talking to that fat, old horse again?"

"Don't listen to him, Elvis. You're still a hunka hunka burning love."

He leaned against the fence beside her. When his jacket brushed aside, she saw that he was carrying his new Glock in a hip holster. He was holding an evergreen wreath in his gloved hand.

"What are you doing with the wreath?" she asked.

"I thought I might tie a red ribbon around it and hang it over the gatepost out front."

Celebrating Christmas was the last thing on her mind. Still, she said, "Good idea. Nicole loves Christmas decorations. When she comes home, she'll be happy to see that wreath."

When she comes home. Carolyn repeated those words to herself. *Nicole will be home for Christmas.*

"Ain't this something?" he said. "With the feds and the choppers and bloodhounds and all."

"Dylan said he'd call out the National Guard if that's what it takes."

They went quiet. She never felt a need to make conversation with Lucas. In the many years she'd known this old cowboy, he'd always been prone to taciturn silence. According to gossip from Polly, Lucas Mann had a reputation as a ladies' man when he went into town, but Carolyn found that characterization hard to imagine.

He shifted his weight from one boot to the other. "You and Burke went over to the Circle M. How'd that turn out?"

Unable to adequately describe her disgust with the Sons of Freedom, she shrugged. "Okay, I guess."

"Logan's not a bad kid, you know."

When she was dating that scumbag, Lucas had been one of the guys who thought she should marry him. "He's changed."

"Betcha he was downright happy to see you."

Why would Lucas make that assumption? "How much do you know about the Sons of Freedom?"

"Not much. They're against the government getting in the way of everyday people. Going back to the good old days."

"When women had fewer rights than cattle?"

"Don't get your panties in a bunch, Carolyn. Ain't nobody fixing to send you back to the kitchen." He lifted the wreath onto his shoulder. "It don't seem like the SOF means any harm."

Not unless you count murder. And whatever

other criminal activities they were engaged in. She'd seen the sophisticated weaponry. Old-time pioneers didn't need automatic assault rifles. "If I ever see Sam Logan again, it'll be too soon."

The front door of the ranch house slammed and she looked toward the sound. Her brother stepped onto the veranda and gripped the railing. Even at this distance, she could see tension weighing down upon him, bending his shoulders.

Giving Elvis a final pat, she hurried back to the house. The closer she got, the more distress she saw in Dylan. When she touched his arm, he was trembling.

His voice was so low she could barely hear him. "We got another call from the kidnapper."

Chapter Twelve

When Dylan was a toddler, two years younger than Carolyn, she hated to see him cry. At the first sign of tears, she'd cuddle him, tell him stories and sing songs until he smiled. If only she could do the same thing now—sweep her brother up in her loving arms and ease the aching in his heart.

She wrapped an arm around his middle and leaned her head on his shoulder. Memories of long-ago lullabies whispered in her mind, but she couldn't bring herself to offer false promises that everything would be all right.

"I told the kidnapper," Dylan said, "that we were having a hard time getting the ransom in time because of the banks. He changed his deadline. We have until Monday at five o'clock."

"That's good news," she said.

"Not for Nicole. She has to be with those bastards for two more days. God only knows what they're doing to her."

Burke joined them on the porch. His manner was subdued but assertive, striking exactly the right tone of calm control. She wondered if that attitude was something they taught at Quantico or if it came naturally.

He said, "You did a good job on the phone, Dylan."

"That's not what I'm thinking," he said darkly. "I'd rather give them the money and get my wife back."

In an ideal world, that was how a negotiation should work. But not with a kidnapper. If Nicole was being held at the Circle M, Logan would never free her—she could identify him. If the pregnant woman, Sunny, was to be believed, Logan had already presided over one murder. Nicole might be the next.

"We have two more days to find her," Carolyn said. "You did good, Dylan. You bought us more time."

"And Dylan got the kidnapper to promise one proof of life a day. More photos of Nicole give us more clues," said Burke.

Thinking of evidence, Carolyn asked, "Did you trace the call?"

"Not this time. He was too fast, and there aren't a lot of cell towers in this area to use for tracking. But it was the same cell phone number as the first call."

"Sheriff Trainer was trying to get information on the phone," she remembered. "Figuring out where the disposable cell was purchased."

"Thus far," Burke said, "he's been unsuccessful."

"And what about Nate Miller?" she asked. "Did the sheriff find anything at his house?"

"Smith joined the sheriff and his deputies for that search. He has nothing good to say about Miller."

"Nobody does," Dylan said. "He's as mean and bitter as his old man."

She agreed with her brother. Being around Miller made her skin crawl. "But did they find evidence?"

"Nothing that links him to the kidnapping, but he doesn't have an alibi for yesterday or last night. We'll keep him on our list of suspects."

A list that was ridiculously long. "Are you talking to other people on that list?"

"Silverman will be coordinating those interviews with Sheriff Trainer." He met her gaze. "As you pointed out when we were in town, a lot of these people won't open up to the FBI. At least they'll talk to Trainer."

The painstaking process of gathering clues frustrated Carolyn. She was a big picture kind of person who made decisions and charged ahead, figuring the details would eventually sort themselves out. "Have you got anything, Burke? Any new leads at all?"

"We're working on it."

In the distance, she saw the helicopter approaching, flying low over the rugged landscape of forest and rock. Dylan gave her a squeeze and separated from her. "There's nothing more I can do here. I'm going up with the chopper while there's still daylight."

She was glad he'd be getting away from the tension-filled house. "I'll be here. If there's nothing I can do to help the investigation, maybe I'll start with some Christmas decorating."

"No," he said firmly. "That's Nicole's job. She loves doing that stuff."

"Should I go in the helicopter with you?" she asked. "Another pair of eyes can't hurt."

"You need to stay here," Burke said. "Corelli is ready to interview you."

She sensed there was something more he wanted to talk to her about. The midnight rendezvous with Sunny? Carolyn needed to be there to reassure Sunny. If that poor girl saw a bunch of FBI guys in bulletproof vests, she'd certainly be spooked.

Waving goodbye to her brother as he ran toward the chopper, she turned to Burke. "Tonight at midnight," she said. "I'm coming with you."

He glanced left and right, looking for spies. The only person she saw was bowlegged Lucas, ambling toward the front gate with the evergreen wreath hanging from his shoulder.

"We'll talk," Burke said. "Inside."

Compared to the chaos of this morning, the dining room had taken on an aura of quiet efficiency.

At one end of the table, Agent Silverman stood before a battery of computers and maps. He wore a phone headset, leaving his hands free to make notes. She'd barely noticed this young man before, probably because he looked like she thought an FBI agent should—totally average. With his brown hair, brown eyes and medium build, Silverman could easily fade into the background. This morning, he'd traded his FBI windbreaker for a faded green Stanford sweatshirt. When she smiled at him, he acknowledged her with a quick grin before he refocused on the task of coordinating the search efforts.

At the opposite end of the table was Corelli, wearing his neat black suit and striped tie. He could have been the junior partner in a law firm.

Burke stood with her behind Corelli's left shoulder. "Take a look at what we've got so far."

Corelli clicked a few keys on his computer, bringing up a rogues' gallery of photographs. "This is what I've found on the names Burke gave me for the SOF."

She scanned the driver's-license photos, recognizing some of the faces from the men she'd seen at the Circle M. The only one who jumped out at her was Butch Thurgood. Even without a Stetson, he looked like a cowboy with a thick, old-fashioned mustache. "Tell me about Butch."

"No criminal record," Corelli said, "but a Web search gave me a lot of info. He's a former rodeo star, a bucking bronc rider. Won the championship title at Cheyenne Frontier Days in 2004 and 2005."

He brought up a full-length photo of Butch Thurgood on the computer screen. A rangy, good-looking man, he wore an embroidered Western shirt and a silver belt buckle the size of a saucer. "He has a reputation as a horse whisperer, somebody who can tame wild mustangs."

Oddly, Carolyn felt reassured. Since Nicole was a veterinarian, she might have something in common with Butch.

Beside her, Burke checked his wristwatch. "Now the bad news. Pete Richter."

Corelli clicked a few keys. The photo that appeared was a police mug shot. His dark eyes had a mean squint. Like Butch, Richter had facial hair but his patchy beard was the result of careless grooming.

"I assume," she said, "that he has a criminal record."

"Starting when he was eighteen," Corelli said. "Shoplifting, vagrancy, DUIs. He served two years in prison for assault."

The reassurance she'd felt when looking at Butch

turned into dread. If Nicole was in the clutches of Richter, things couldn't be good. "What about the rest of the SOF men?"

"Minor charges, here and there. One dishonorable discharge from the military. They're low-level, petty criminals," Burke said. "Amazingly, Sam Logan has a clean record, apart from one arrest for fraud that never resulted in trial because the woman he'd stolen from dropped the charges."

She wasn't surprised. "Logan can be charming."

Burke scoffed, "Ready for more information?"

"I suppose."

He waved his hand like a magician going for the big reveal. "Okay, Corelli. Show her the money."

The Sons of Freedom bank statement appeared on the screen.

"Wait a minute." Carolyn averted her gaze. "Can you do this without a warrant? Is this even legal?"

"Corelli knows how to follow protocol and he's a talented hacker."

On the screen, she read the balance in the account. "One thousand two hundred dollars? How can Logan support all those people on that amount? There must be another account."

"Nope," Burke said. "No other account in Sam Logan's name. Nothing else for the SOF."

"Credit cards? Loans?"

"Nothing."

Corelli flipped through a series of other financial

documents while he explained, "Here's how it works. Before a bill comes due, Logan deposits just enough money—in cash—to cover the check. *Always in cash.*"

Finances were Carolyn's area of expertise. When taking on a new supplier for Carlisle Certified Organic Beef, she carefully reviewed all their financial documents. "Seems like a clever way to avoid paying taxes. If he only balances out with small amounts, he can claim it all comes from contributions."

"Good insight," Burke said. "Source of income is the important factor. It's hard to know exactly how the SOF makes their money when everything is on a cash basis."

"I'm not a forensic accountant," Corelli said, "but I feel safe in assuming that Logan has a boatload of cash that isn't banked."

"That might explain the security cameras," she said, "and the heavy-duty firepower at the SOF compound. They're afraid of being robbed."

Burke raised a skeptical eyebrow. "Let's not characterize Logan as a little old man who stuffs his mattress with ten-dollar bills. He needs his guards to keep his business secret, to protect his little kingdom."

"From what?"

"Feds like me," Burke said. "Whatever he's buying and selling is illegal. Could be weapons, could be drugs, could be any number of black-market items that would be highly interesting to the DEA or Homeland Security."

Though Carolyn agreed that Logan was probably involved in some kind of illegal activity, she didn't think of her former fiancé as a terrorist. "Logan isn't that clever."

"He's no mastermind," Burke agreed. "But he could be working for one. His compound could be one stop on a distribution chain."

She didn't like the picture he was painting, especially didn't like the thought that Nicole might be in the middle of this spider's web. Not to mention the other innocent women and children.

They needed to get everyone out of there, starting tonight with Sunny.

TWELVE MINUTES BEFORE the midnight meet with Sunny, Burke lay on his belly in the cold, dead grass outside the west field bordering the Circle M. He peered through infrared, heat-sensing binoculars at a stand of pine trees, watching for any sign of movement. From this vantage point, he couldn't see any of the buildings of the SOF compound. Except for the clump of pines, this field was flat and feature-less.

Carolyn crouched beside him, hiding behind the bared branches of a shrub. His backup—Neville and Silverman—were both heavily armed. They'd separated and found their own hiding spots, fading into the landscape. The only way Burke could see them was through the heat-sensing binoculars.

He didn't like this setup. With very little cover, they were exposed to the possibility of ambush. If Logan and his men charged toward them on horseback, escape would be difficult. They'd parked a couple of hundred yards away, and he didn't like their chances for a safe retreat if they were outnumbered and attacked with a barrage of bullets from semiautomatic weapons.

He especially hated that Carolyn was here. She'd insisted on being part of this operation, dug in her heels. He'd wanted to pull rank, reminding her that he was in charge. But her argument made too much sense. If, in fact, Sunny truly wanted to escape from the Circle M, she'd be alarmed if she didn't see Carolyn—the person she trusted.

He glanced toward his companion. Dressed all in black, she was as slender as a shadow. "I'd feel a whole lot better if you were wearing full body armor, like Neville and Silverman."

"This bulletproof vest is enough," she said quietly. "The whole reason I'm here is to keep Sunny from being scared. If she sees me dressed like a robot, she'll run."

Again, her logic made sense. For exactly the same reason she'd stated, Burke was only wearing a Kevlar vest. "Let's go over the plan again."

"It's not that complicated," she said. "I stay with you. When you give me the go-ahead, I run to the trees. No time for conversation. I take Sunny by the hand and bring her back here."

"If you hear me call out a warning, what do you do?"

"Seek cover." She turned so she was looking at the flat land between their hiding spot and the pines. "There isn't much to hide behind."

"Hit the dirt," he said. "The main thing is not to stand and run, making yourself a big, fat target."

"Excuse me? You think I'm big and fat?"

"Your body's great."

"Do you really think so?"

"I like the way you're put together." This wasn't the right time for this conversation, but he couldn't control his thoughts. Even now, in the midst of a life-threatening situation, his brain flashed snapshots of Carolyn. The swing of her hips when he followed her up the staircase. Her long legs striding with purpose. Her casual grace when she sat on her bed. "Oh, yeah. You've got a great body."

"You're no slouch yourself," she said. "Do you work out or do you get enough exercise chasing the evildoers of the world?"

He didn't answer, preferring to concentrate on the business at hand. After a moment of silence, he lowered his binoculars and checked his wristwatch. Five minutes until midnight.

"I've been thinking," she said, "about Logan being part of a distribution chain."

He peered through his binoculars again. "And?"

"If somebody is bringing illegal goods into this area, the most logical route would be the pass that follows that old Indian Trail. It comes out of the mountains at the south pasture where all the sabotage was taking place."

After studying topographical maps of the area, he'd been leaning toward the same conclusion. He and Corelli had been listening to the chatter from Logan's office where Burke had hidden a bug. There had been talk about making a pickup, but no one mentioned where or what would be delivered. "You could be right about the route."

"The sabotage started after Dylan moved the herd into that pasture."

"Logan and his men might have been causing trouble so Dylan would move the cattle. If they're using that trail, there's less chance that someone would see them if the pasture was empty."

"We can't tell Dylan about this," she whispered. "He's already blaming himself for Nicole's kidnapping. Lucas kept telling him to move the cattle."

A suspicious note in her voice caused him to lower the binoculars and look toward her. "What else are you thinking?"

"Nothing really." She shook her head. "Forget it."

She'd mentioned the foreman—Lucas Mann.

Was there something more sinister behind his warning to move the herd? Was Lucas the traitor? He knew that Carolyn would find it hard to accuse that bowlegged cowboy, a trusted employee who had worked at the ranch for years.

Burke was less sanguine about the foreman's loyalty. Lucas could have been bribed; he had enough extra cash to buy that new Glock, which wasn't a cheap weapon. "Is there something you want to tell me about Lucas?"

"I said forget it."

Lucas had been in the house when somebody took the phone number from her cell. He'd also discovered the fire at the stable and acted quickly to rescue the horses. Could he be responsible for setting that blaze?

Burke looked up at the waning moon and a sky sprinkled with a multitude of stars—thousands of tiny spotlights. That beautiful, clear night sky worked to their disadvantage. He would have preferred cloud cover, even snow.

Aiming his heat-sensing binoculars again, he picked out a figure, moving slowly. "She's coming."

Carolyn peered though the dark. "I don't see her."

"Looks like she's alone. Let's get closer."

He traded his binoculars for night vision goggles. Bent low, they crept across the field. He clearly saw the blond pregnant woman in a long dress and a parka. She walked carefully, pausing every few steps to look back over her shoulder. Her hand rested protectively on her swollen belly. Her apparent fear seemed to indicate that she wasn't part of an ambush, which led Burke to his next worry: Was someone coming after her?

He hoped that Sunny was clever enough to avoid being caught by the surveillance cameras.

"I see her," Carolyn said. "She's almost to the trees."

"It doesn't appear that anybody is following. Go quick."

She darted across the last stretch of open field. For tonight's operation, Carolyn had exchanged her cowboy boots for running shoes. She moved with admirable stealth, standing when she reached the trees.

Through his goggles, he saw the two women meet. Carolyn wrapped her arm around Sunny and pulled her forward. Instead of running, they came toward him slowly.

Still no sign of pursuit.

Burke hurried forward and joined them. Sunny clung to Carolyn's arm. Her face contorted.

"I could use a little help," Carolyn said.

"Is she injured?"

"You need to carry her, Burke."

"What's wrong?"

"She's in labor."

Chapter Thirteen

Burke's jaw dropped. He froze, standing in the middle of the open field between escape and the Circle M. He'd just warned Carolyn not to do what he was doing. *Don't just stand here like a big, fat target.* A successful hostage extraction required stealth and cunning. *Not babies.*

"In labor," he said. "Right now?"

"Yes," Carolyn hissed. Though she was making a valiant effort to hold Sunny upright, the young woman's knees folded. In slow motion, she sank to the ground, dragging Carolyn with her in a tangle of limbs. Through clenched teeth, Sunny emitted a sound that was something between a creaking door hinge and a feral growl.

"Help her." Carolyn bounced to her feet and punched him in the arm. "She's not going to make it to the car by herself."

He handed his night goggles and gun to Carolyn, then squatted beside Sunny. She gasped and her belly heaved. Her face was pale and round and scared.

He needed to reassure her. "Um, congratulations."

"Burke," Carolyn snapped, "pick her up."

"Right." He got down close to Sunny. "I'm going to carry you, okay? Can you put your arm around my neck?"

"Yes," she whispered, "thank you."

Holding her under the arms and at the knees, he lifted her off the ground. Her weight wasn't too much; he could easily bench-press two-fifty. But Sunny's body was awkward—regular-sized arms and legs attached to a ripe watermelon.

From the SOF compound, he heard a shout. A woman's voice. "Sunny? Where are you, Sunny?"

"It's Sharon," Sunny said. "She's supposed to keep an eye on us at night."

They needed to make tracks, but he couldn't exactly break into a sprint with a pregnant woman in his arms. Though this field was flat, the ground was rocky. He didn't want to stumble.

"How close are the contractions?" Carolyn asked as they lurched forward.

"It wasn't bad until just a little while ago."

"There's nothing to worry about." Carolyn's voice was soft and gentle. "Just keep breathing. Try to relax."

Relax? Was she joking? He wasn't sure how

Sunny felt, but he was operating under red alert panic.

Other voices joined the woman who had been calling Sunny's name. Other people were looking for her. If the gang at the compound checked their surveillance cameras, they'd know which direction to go. The men would be armed. Burke could already sense the bullet piercing his back.

"Silverman," he snarled into the darkness. "Neville."

The two men in full body armor, goggles and helmets rose from their sniper's nests in the field and jogged silently toward them.

When Sunny saw them, her eyes popped wide. "Oh, my God."

"It's okay," Burke said. "They're with us."

"They're from outer space." She struggled in his arms. "Am I being abducted by aliens?"

Silverman flipped up his goggles. "I'm a person. See?"

"Settle down." Burke gave her a shake, hoping her brain would engage. "You're safe now."

"I don't feel safe."

"Trust me," he ordered. "Can you do that?"

She groaned, "Okay."

"I'm taking her to the car," Burke said to his men as he staggered toward the trees. On the other side, their van was parked. "Stay back and cover our retreat."

"They have flashlights," Carolyn said. "They're coming this way."

He wanted to make sure Neville and Silverman knew they had to hold fire as long as possible. There were still innocent hostages at the Circle M, and he couldn't take a chance on anyone getting hurt.

"Don't shoot unless—"

He couldn't speak. Sunny's arm had clenched around his neck in a stranglehold. Her body had gone into a spasm.

Only twenty more yards and they'd be in the shelter of the forest.

"Keep breathing," Carolyn whispered.

He gasped. "Thanks."

"I wasn't talking to you, Burke."

His forward progress stopped. He kneeled, fearful that he was going to drop her. Sunny's contraction caused her to stiffen. She bit her lower lip to keep from crying out, and he appreciated the effort. If the SOF searchers found them, they might open fire. Definitely not optimum circumstances for delivering a baby.

As soon as she calmed down, he summoned all his strength and ran into the forest. Beneath the sheltering branches, he turned to look behind them. He saw flashlights bobbing on the opposite side of the field.

They were a good distance away. He hoped they

wouldn't connect Sunny's disappearance with him or the Carlisle's.

"Almost safe," he said to Sunny.

"Hurry."

They moved in a clump toward the van. Silverman dashed past them and slid open the rear door. Burke set the pregnant woman inside. Before he could go around to the driver's side, she grabbed his jacket.

The strength of her grip astonished him. He wanted to peel her clinging hands off him, wanted to leave her in Carolyn's care. But Sunny's wide eyes pleaded. "Stay with me," she said. "You told me to trust you."

"I did say that." And how the hell could he refuse a woman in labor? He reconfigured the third row of seats into a long bench and climbed in beside her. "Carolyn, you drive."

Neville took the passenger seat. Silverman sat in the middle seats. They took off.

The immediate danger seemed to have passed. They had successfully extracted a hostage from the Sons of Freedom compound. But nobody in the van was breathing a sigh of relief.

Without turning on the headlights, Carolyn drove as fast as she could along a rutted dirt road. Burke sat with his back against the window. Sunny leaned against his chest with her legs stretched out in front of her. She groaned as Carolyn jolted over a deep furrow. "I want my mom."

"Later, you can call her," Burke said as he pulled out his cell phone. "First, we contact your doctor."

"Don't have one. Logan said we don't need doctors. We're like the pioneers, using natural herbs and stuff."

"Are you telling me that the children at the compound don't get vaccinations? No checkups?"

"I know it's not right," Sunny sighed.

It sure as hell wasn't. In his book, the lack of medical care at the SOF compound amounted to child abuse. "Do the others want to leave the Circle M?"

"Most of the women do," Sunny said. "But we don't know where to go. We've got no money. Nothing but these ugly clothes. At least Logan makes sure we all get fed."

"How long have you lived there?"

She stroked her belly. "Nine months. I thought I was in love with Butch Thurgood, but he's as rotten as the rest of them."

In the middle seat, Silverman had taken off his helmet, goggles and much of his body armor. He leaned between the seats. "See? I'm not an alien."

Not an alien. Just an idiot. "She understands, Silverman."

"I didn't mean to insult you," Sunny said. "I was just, you know, confused. You looked really scary in the moonlight."

"My name is Mike." He reached back and

touched her leg. "You're going to be fine. Everything's going to be fine."

With a sweet smile, she said, "Thank you, Mike."

Oh, sure. Thank him. He didn't carry you across the field. Burke was pretty sure that he deserved a medal—at least a written commendation—for his actions tonight. At the very least, he wanted to get some useful information from Sunny.

"You told Carolyn about a murder," he prompted.

"Lisa's sister. Her name was Barbara."

"Last name?"

"I think it's Ayers. None of the women use their last names. We're supposed to be part of a new family."

Stripping away identity was a typical technique for handling hostages. "What's your last name, Sunny?"

"Lansky. Sunny Rebecca Lansky."

"That's good." He gave her a little hug. "Tell me about the murder."

"It was awful."

Carolyn drove onto a paved road and turned on the headlights. She hit the accelerator and said loudly, "Burke, this might not be the time to have this talk."

"I want to tell him," Sunny said.

But she went rigid in his arms. She'd suffered quietly in the field, but there was no longer a need to hold back.

"Go ahead," Burke said. "If you want to yell, go ahead."

She grabbed his hand and let out an earsplitting screech. From the middle seat, Silverman coached her. "Hang in there, Sunny. You can do it. Do you know the breathing? Hee-hee. Hoo-hoo."

The screech continued. Nothing hee-hee about it.

"She's not having the baby now," Burke snapped.

"She could," Silverman said.

"Oh. Hell. No. She's waiting until we get to the hospital." In the meantime, she was crushing his fingers into pulp. "Hold it in, Sunny."

"Doesn't work that way," Silverman said. "When it's time, it's time."

"Since when are you a midwife?"

"I helped my sister give birth. I know all about this stuff."

Sunny went quiet, breathing heavily. Her grip on his hand relaxed. "Barbara wanted to leave the SOF. She never really wanted to be there in the first place. She only stayed because of her sister. Lisa has a drug problem."

"What about you? Drug problem?"

"No." She shook her head. "I never got into drugs."

Sunny seemed like a decent kid, even though she was kind of a mess with her blond hair growing out at the roots and her baggy dress with long woolen leggings. "Are there drugs at the Circle M?"

"Some kind of supposedly herbal supplement. I never took it. Because of the baby."

"Good for you," Burke said. "Tell me about Barbara."

"She found out she was pregnant, too. We talked about leaving together. When we told Logan we wanted to go, he got really mad. He reminded us what it's like on the outside for a single mother. No friends. No money."

"There's always someone," Silverman said. He maneuvered around and stretched out his arm to dab her forehead with a red kerchief. "Somebody who will step up and—"

"Do something useful," Burke ordered. "Call the Delta hospital and tell them we're coming."

"Sunny needs to know there's a support system."

Agent Mike Silverman was usually an efficient operative who had no problem with following orders. Something about being around a pregnant woman had messed with his head. "Make the damn call."

Glaring at Burke, he pulled out his cell phone. Since Carolyn was driving at about a thousand miles an hour, they ought to be at the hospital in minutes. "Okay, Sunny. Both you and Barbara wanted to leave. Then what?"

"Her baby's daddy was Pete Richter. A real bastard. She made the mistake of talking to him. I saw him slap her really hard. She was unconscious.

I wanted to help her. Really, I did. But I was scared."

"You're safe now," Burke assured her. He wanted to get the whole story before her next contraction. "What happened next? Give me the short version."

"Richter and Logan dragged Barbara off into the barn, and I never saw her again. Logan told us she ran away."

"But you didn't believe him."

"She never would have left without saying goodbye to Lisa. A couple of days later, I was out walking. Not far from the trees where you came and got me, I found a plot of fresh-turned earth. I know that's where they buried her."

It would have been neater if Sunny had actually witnessed the murder. Finding the body would be useful, but it wouldn't tell them who killed Barbara Ayers.

"New topic," Burke said. "Can you tell me anything about the woman who was kidnapped? Nicole Carlisle?"

"I never saw her."

"Is there a place at the Circle M where they could hide her?"

"Plenty of places. Root cellars. Trailers." She shrugged.

Burke pressed for a more definitive answer. "If Butch and Richter were holding Nicole captive, where would they be?"

"There's a trailer behind the bunkhouse where a lot of couples go to make love. Butch didn't like it. He wanted more privacy. He took me to this place. We had to ride on the Indian Trail to get there." Her voice broke. "It was springtime, just starting to warm up. It felt like he loved me. Everything was so beautiful."

"Where was this place?"

"A shallow cave that looks out over the mountains and valleys. Right above the Cathedral Rocks with all the spikes and spires."

She grabbed his hand. "Here comes another one."

"So soon?"

"Four minutes apart," Silverman announced.

"How far are we from the damn hospital?"

"Not far," Carolyn yelled over her shoulder. "We're almost in Delta."

Sunny let out a long wail. Her knees drew up and separated as if she was ready to shoot out the baby.

Silverman held out his hand, and she latched on to him, too.

"Don't push," he said. "We're almost to the hospital."

"Did you hear that?" Burke whispered in her ear. "No pushing."

Sunny ended the contraction with short, huffing gasps. "I need my mom."

"Absolutely. No problem." Burke waved his cell phone. "You can call her. Where does she live?"

"Mom," She sobbed, "doesn't even know I'm pregnant."

Burke held the phone in front of her. "Tell me the number."

"No time. I want this baby out of me."

Carolyn whipped into the emergency entrance for the hospital and leaped from the car. In seconds, two guys in scrubs had loaded Sunny onto a gurney. Silverman went with them into the hospital.

Burke leaned against the van and exhaled a long breath.

Carolyn stood beside him. In the harsh light outside the E.R. entrance, he saw her smirk. "That went well."

In spite of her sarcasm, he was pleased with the way his team had extracted Sunny—a witness who had given them useful information against Logan.

While they were at the hospital, they'd checked on Jesse Longbridge. Burke hoped for a lucky break. If the bodyguard was out of his coma, he could identify the men who kidnapped Nicole.

Chapter Fourteen

Hospital visiting hours had, of course, ended much earlier. And the nurses didn't seem pleased about the after-midnight exception they made for Carolyn and Burke after he showed his FBI credentials.

Walking beside him down a clean corridor, she tried to keep her sneakers from squeaking on the tile floor. Her hands were washed, but the black clothes she'd worn for the meeting with Sunny were filthy and sweaty. She felt like a germ invading sterile territory.

Hospitals made her uncomfortable, especially this one—it was where her father had passed away. She shouldn't be here, shouldn't really be involved in anything like a hostage extraction. She was a CEO, not part of the CIA. But the alternative was doing nothing, and she had to admit that rescuing Sunny had been a rush. Escaping from pursuit and racing to the hospital made her feel like she was accomplishing something. And it looked like there would be a happy ending to that story. Sunny was already in the delivery room with Silverman. If only they could rescue Nicole so easily, Carolyn could get back to her regular life—a life that didn't include Special Agent J. D. Burke.

She wasn't exactly sure how she felt about never seeing him again. Like her, he was dressed in black—a color that should have made him appear smaller. But he looked huge and dangerous. His jaw was tight. His dark eyes burned with a purposeful intensity that fascinated her.

Perhaps she'd miss him.

At the end of the hall, they entered Jesse Longbridge's private room. Wentworth and another guard from Longbridge Security greeted them with a handshake and stepped aside.

Dim night-lights gave the room an ethereal quality. Jesse lay motionless and unconscious under a white sheet. IV lines ran into the veins in his right arm. The left was bandaged. A large dressing covered his left shoulder. A nasal cannula delivered oxygen to his lungs, but he was breathing on his own. His chest rose and fell steadily. The heart monitor made a regular beep.

As Carolyn approached his bed, she felt a strong connection to this man who was, in fact, a stranger. They'd never been introduced, but his blood had flowed through her fingers and stained her clothing. She gently brushed his thick black hair off his forehead. He was rather handsome. She'd heard that Jesse was half Navajo and could see his heritage in his strong features. His eyelashes flickered, and she thought for a moment that he would waken. But the slight movement faded into stillness.

Concentrating, she sent positive thoughts from her brain to his. *You're going to get better, Jesse. You will be well again.* He'd risked his life trying to protect Nicole. Frankly, he was the answer to all their questions. When he woke, he'd be able to identify the kidnappers.

Seeing him lying there—so still and quiet—saddened her. He didn't deserve these injuries. He was one of the good guys, someone who tried to do the right thing. And how was he repaid for his efforts? *Damn it, this wasn't fair.*

Burke stood close behind her. "He's expected to make a full recovery."

That knowledge didn't assuage her anger. "What if he doesn't?"

"He will."

She turned her head. In Burke's expression she saw strength and determination, but he couldn't affect Jesse's medical condition. Some things were simply out of his control. And hers, too.

Quietly, she stepped away from Jesse's bed. Wentworth accompanied her and Burke, leaving the other guard in the room to keep watch. He led them past the nurse's station into a private office with file cabinets, a computer and a couple of chairs. Wentworth closed the door.

Burke asked, "What's the update on Jesse's condition?"

"Same as before. No broken bones. No organ damage. All his systems are functioning and he's got brain activity. A couple of times, he's opened his eyes, looked around and then zonked out again. The docs say he'll be okay."

"I'm sure he will be." Burke took his cell phone from his pocket, checked the caller ID and excused himself. "Sorry, I have to take this call."

"Thank you, Wentworth," Carolyn said, "for all you've done."

"It's my job, ma'am."

"Can you explain to me why Jesse isn't awake?"

"There's no medical explanation, ma'am. But I'll tell you this. Jesse's no slacker. When he decides to wake up, I guarantee he'll be raring to go."

Though Wentworth was obviously concerned, he kept his fears to himself. His stoicism reminded Carolyn of the cowboy ethic. Never show emotion.

She wanted to scream, to jump up and down and rail against the bastards who had put this good man in the hospital.

"Is there anything I can do?" she asked. "Should we call in a specialist?"

"Jesse's getting first-rate care," Wentworth said. "It helps to have two of us here, 24/7. We're also keeping tabs on your ransom money."

Swept up in concern for Jesse, she'd almost forgotten that the ransom had been delivered here to the hospital so the traitor at the ranch wouldn't know the money had arrived. A million dollars in cash! How could she forget? "It's in a backpack?"

"Yes, ma'am. A real big backpack."

Burke completed his call and rejoined them. Without missing a beat, he said. "We'll be taking the ransom with us."

"Yes, sir."

Burke slipped easily into the leadership role. Though he wasn't Wentworth's boss or his client, he still commanded respect. The only time she'd seen that fierce composure slip was with Sunny. Handling a woman in labor had dumbfounded Special Agent Burke.

He turned to her. "That was Corelli on the phone. Logan has called the ranch twice, looking for you. It's worth finding out what he wants."

"It's probably about Sunny."

"Most likely," Burke said. "If he tries to contact you again, Corelli will patch the call through to my phone."

"Okay." She didn't want to talk to Logan, but Burke was right. She might learn something useful.

"Wentworth," Burke said, "I've got another assignment for you. We have another witness at the hospital who needs a full-time guard. She'll be in the maternity wing."

Though Wentworth nodded, he said, "Could be a problem, sir. There are only two of us, and we need to take turns sleeping and watching Jesse."

"I'm leaving an FBI agent here with you."

"Silverman?" she asked.

"He might as well stay here," Burke said. "You saw how he was fawning all over Sunny."

"I thought he was sweet," she said.

Burke turned to Wentworth. "Can you manage with three guards?"

"I'll work it out, sir."

"Actually," Carolyn said, "you'll be watching three people. Jesse, Sunny and a newborn baby."

Burke's cell phone rang. He checked the ID and handed it to her. "It's Logan. Don't tell him anything about Sunny."

She took the phone from him and answered, "What do you want?"

"I knew you'd be awake," he said. "There are probably a half dozen feds monitoring the phones. Did they get you out of bed? Are you wearing one of those skimpy little nightshirts? I remember a blue one with butterflies."

A shudder of revulsion went through her. She hated that he knew what she wore to bed. "Why did you call?"

"Where's Sunny?"

"Who? What are you talking about?"

"Sunny," he repeated. "She was one of the women you were talking to today. She ran off, and I'm pretty damn sure she came to you for help."

From the way he was talking, she didn't think he'd actually seen them rescuing Sunny. It would be useful to know if any of those people with flashlights had spotted them. "Why would you think she came to me?"

"Because you put ideas in her head. I know how you are."

He knew nothing about her. And, apparently, nothing about their hostage extraction. She gave a short laugh and said, "You think I poisoned her mind? Convinced her to leave you?"

"That's right."

"In case you hadn't noticed," she said, "I kind of have my hands full. Why would I care about some woman who was dumb enough to join up with you in the first place?"

"Like you," he reminded her. "You used to be with me."

"Thank God I came to my senses."

"Where else would Sunny run to? She came to your ranch," he said. "You should know that she's a liar. A runaway that I picked up off the streets. You can't believe a word she says."

"She's not at the ranch, Logan."

"Don't mess with me."

"Or else?" She laughed again, harshly. "What are you going to do?"

"You think you're untouchable. You're the high-and-mighty Carolyn Carlisle. But I know how to bring you down."

Was he talking about Nicole? Would he hurt Nicole to get back at her? "Are you threatening me? Again?"

"Take it any way you want."

The phone went dead.

AN HOUR LATER, sitting in the passenger seat of the van, Carolyn had pushed aside her sadness about Jesse and her frustrated anger at Logan. Her mind filled with happier images as she thought about Sunny's beautiful baby girl. After their wild ride to get her to the hospital, the actual delivery—assisted by Silverman—had been uncomplicated and fast. And the result?

Carolyn grinned. Sunny had given birth to a perfect little being with wise, curious eyes and rosebud lips.

She sighed. "Babies are so miraculous."

"Yeah," Burke said. "Bundles of joy."

"Come on, tough guy. I saw your face when you were holding the baby. You liked it."

"Don't confuse me with Silverman." He frowned at the road ahead. "I don't know what the hell's gotten into him. He's single, never married. What does he know about babies?"

"More than you," she teased.

The atmosphere between them was different tonight—more intimate. In the dark, when she couldn't see clearly, her other senses were heightened, as if she could hear him breathing and feel the warmth emanating from his body. His voice seemed more resonant; the tones vibrated inside her.

They'd experienced so much in one day. The emotional high of rescuing Sunny. And the low point this morning when she broke down in tears. In some ways, Burke knew her more thoroughly than men she'd dated for years. But she still didn't have much of an inkling of his background. Now—when they were finally alone—was her time to find out about him.

"Did you have siblings?" she asked.

"I was an only child, raised in Chicago by a single mom."

She was surprised that he'd offered so much biographical information—a whole sentence. Usually, he answered her questions with a question of his own. She pressed for more. "You grew up in the city?"

"Mostly."

Pulling answers from him was like sucking on a bent straw. "Does that mean you also lived somewhere else?"

"I spent a lot of summers in rural Wisconsin with my grandparents. That's where I learned how to ride."

He yawned. She knew that his defenses were down. "After high school, what did you do?"

"Is there a point to your questions?"

"I'm trying to get to know you," she said.

"Why?"

"Because I like you, Burke."

As the words left her lips, her heart took a little jump. She wasn't usually so direct; Carolyn knew how to play the dating game. But there wasn't time for them to do the traditional get-to-know-you dance. For them, there would be no candlelit dinners or long walks in the park. They didn't even have time for a first date.

If anything was going to happen between them, it had to be as fast and furious as a tornado. *Is that what I want? To be swept up in a wild vortex?* She reminded herself that tornadoes were generally looked upon as disasters.

"You like me," he said.

Lights from the dashboard showed a grin that was a bit too arrogant for her taste. She backtracked, not wanting to give him an edge. "Maybe I do."

"Maybe?" He turned his head and gave her a cocky look—a challenge that made her want to raise the stakes.

"When I first met you," she said, "I thought you were an insensitive, domineering jerk."

"And now?"

"You're sensitive enough." And sexier than she wanted to admit. "The problem is that I don't know you well enough to form much of an opinion."

"Fine," he said. "Ask your questions."

"You said you were once in love. Tell me about that."

"I was a first-year law student," he said. "She was my professor. Beautiful and tough, she was the smartest person I've ever known. I couldn't stay away from her." He sighed. "I wanted to be with her, even after she told me about her illness."

His voice had deepened, lending weight to his words.

"What did she have?" Carolyn asked.

"An inoperable brain aneurysm. For most of her life, she faced the knowledge that she could die at any moment. We lived together for six months. Then she was gone."

The tragedy was still with him. She could feel his sorrow. "I'm sorry, Burke."

"I dropped out of law school and joined the Chicago P.D. Stayed there for five years. My mom was killed in a car accident, and I moved to the FBI." He shrugged. "That's it. My life story."

A story of love and loss. No wonder he was so guarded. "How did you become a hostage negotiator?"

"The FBI decided that's where I fit. You'll have

to ask profilers, like Smith and Silverman, for the psychological details."

She didn't need more explanation. He'd trusted her. He'd shared his past. And that was enough.

Through the windshield, she saw the lights of the ranch house. Though it was after two o'clock in the morning, someone was still awake. Not Dylan, she hoped. Her brother needed more sleep. "Is Corelli still monitoring the equipment?"

"That's his job," Burke said. "He's listening to the bug I left in Logan's office. It'll be interesting to hear what they have to say about Sunny's disappearance, especially after your conversation with him."

And Logan's threat. "I could have handled that better."

"You did fine."

She looked toward the house. After this brief reprieve, they were returning to the crucible. Tension tied a knot in her gut. She wanted more respite, wanted to be with Burke, wanted their intimacy to increase. She wanted to spend the rest of the night in the safety of his arms. *Am I ready to make love to him? Is he ready?*

Carolyn pushed the thought away. "Why did you want to bring the ransom with us?"

"It doesn't do much good to have the money if we can't deliver."

"I'm surprised," she said. He'd been consistently

opposed to handing over the ransom. "You're thinking of paying the kidnappers?"

"Only if there's no other way."

She wouldn't miss the money. All she wanted was for Nicole to be back home. Safe.

Chapter Fifteen

After they parked, Carolyn followed Burke into the house. He carried the massive backpack over his shoulder. Not exactly a subtle way of transporting the ransom, but it couldn't be helped. They went immediately to her brother's office and closed the door. Carolyn knew exactly where to stash the money.

"My father had this safe installed ten years ago," she said. "We'd had a couple of robberies and he was worried about the amount of cash we keep on hand."

"Is the safe big enough for this backpack?"

"Oh, yeah."

She pulled the window curtains tight, remembering the day when her father brought her and Dylan into his office and told them that no one—absolutely no one—was to know the combination to his safe. No one except for Dylan and herself.

Thinking back, she realized that he was probably overreacting. "Dad wanted a safe that was large enough to hold our cash on hand and the most valuable pieces of art that my mother had picked up."

"You said that she runs an art gallery in Manhattan, right?"

"Mom has amazing taste. Very expensive taste. For a while, Dad locked up the Gorman sculptures and the paintings by Georgia O'Keefe." She gestured to a priceless Charles Russell painting of a cowboy roping a steer above the leather couch. "I convinced him that art was supposed to be seen. If he wasn't going to put those paintings on the wall, he might as well send them to my mom."

She unfastened two hidden latches on a bookcase. It swung open like a door on well-oiled hinges. The wall safe behind it was five feet tall.

"Excellent," Burke said. "The money should be safe in there."

She twirled the combination lock and opened the safe. There was plenty of room inside. As soon as Burke deposited the backpack, she closed the steel door and returned the bookcase to its original position. For now, the million-dollar ransom was secure.

She turned and faced Burke. He leaned against her brother's desk with his arms folded across his broad chest.

"About those questions you asked in the car," he said.

"Yes?"

"Did I pass your test?"

"I wasn't—"

"Sure you were. You're checking me out, trying to decide what to do about this attraction we're both feeling. Don't deny it, Carolyn."

"It's what I do," she said without apology. "I gather information, make decisions and take action."

"You're an effective businesswoman. No doubt about that."

But was she so skillful when it came to more personal decisions? She tried to make an assessment. From the way he conducted his life and the way he coped with his past, she assumed that he was a good man. Decent. Strong. A leader. But not someone she'd look to for a long-term relationship. He definitely wasn't a man who wanted to settle down and have babies. "You've been honest with me."

"I have."

His smile drew her closer. There was no logical way to analyze the magnetism between them. She couldn't explain the sensual shivers that prickled the hairs on her arms. Nor could she deny them. "You're a man I can trust."

She approached him, deliberately unfolded his arms and stepped into his embrace. Then, she kissed him.

Without hesitation, he responded. His mouth was hot and demanding. He closed his arms around her, enveloped her, dominated her, held her so tightly that he took her breath away.

Carolyn reeled in his arms, unaccustomed to such fierce passion. Her leg wrapped around his thigh, squeezing hard, rubbing against him. Arousal spread through her like wildfire. She wanted more from him. Demanded it.

He tore off her jacket, discarded it on the floor of the office and peeled off his own. Her hands dove under his black turtleneck and climbed his chest, reveling in the touch of crisp hair and hard muscle. Kissing him again, her arms encircled him. Her fingers clutched at his back.

A deep growl emanated from his throat, and she met that primitive sound with a moan of her own. No more time for thought. Only action.

He swung her around so she was pressed against the desk, and she was glad for the support. He yanked her shirt over her head. In a deft move, he unhooked her bra. He tugged at her barrette and her hair cascaded out of the ponytail.

For a moment he paused. His dark eyes slid over her body, naked from the waist up. "Beautiful," he murmured.

Slowly and purposefully, he cupped her breasts and lowered his head to suckle at her rose-colored nipples.

Her back arched. She bared her throat as a burst of pleasure exploded inside her.

He went lower, trailing his clever tongue along the center line of her torso. Her belt was open. He unfastened the top button of her jeans.

Breathing hard, she slithered through his grasp and sank to the floor in front of the desk. No way would she be the only person naked in this equation.

"Your shirt," she growled. "Take it off."

"You like to give orders."

"I like to be obeyed."

When he took off his shirt, she stared, unabashed. Oh yes, he was something else. Big. Strong. Gorgeous.

She lay back on the woven Navajo rug. "Now your jeans."

"You're going first."

Teasing, he tugged at her jeans while she made a halfhearted effort to keep them on. This was a battle of wills that she had no intention of winning.

Finally, their clothes were gone. He lowered himself on top of her. The sensation of flesh meeting flesh created a friction unlike anything she'd ever experienced. Burke matched her passion and overwhelmed her.

He drew away from her and reached for his jeans. "I need a condom."

"It's okay. I'm on the pill." In his eyes, she saw

a hint of hesitation. "Damn it, Burke. I'm clean. This is the safest sex you'll ever have."

"There's nothing safe about you, lady."

He was right about that. Nothing safe about either one of them.

Burke hadn't come to the Carlisle Ranch to make friends, and he never expected to find a lover. Her long, sexy legs wrapped around him. Her arms held him tight. Before he realized what she was doing, she'd rolled over so she was on top, straddling him. In control.

Oh hell, no. He wanted more from her before he reached climax.

He pulled her back down and rolled again. He looked down into her fascinating green eyes. Her lips parted. He covered her mouth with his own, stealing her breath.

She turned her head away. Her body writhed beneath him. "Now," she demanded.

"Not yet."

His need had grown to an almost unbearable level, but he intended to make this moment into something she'd remember for the rest of her life. Paying careful, sensual attention to every part of her body, he brought her to the shivering edge of climax.

"Please," she gasped. "Please, Burke."

"Since you ask so politely…"

He entered her with a hard thrust. She drew him

tighter, tighter. The time for game playing was over. He couldn't hold back for one more second. Driven by a primal need, the fierce rhythm of their lovemaking raced, fast and furious, until they exploded together.

He collapsed onto the rug beside her, holding her trembling body against him.

There was no need for words.

Finally, he and Carolyn were in total agreement.

Gradually he became aware of the reality of their surroundings. They were lying on a woven rug on a hard floor. The air was chilly. He kissed the top of her head. Her black hair was soft and smelled like spring flowers. "Carolyn?"

She responded with a muffled sound and snuggled closer.

"Carolyn, are you asleep?"

He separated from her and looked down. Her eyes were closed. A contented smile curved her lips. He studied her face in a way she'd never allow if she'd been awake and scrappy. In the smooth curve of her forehead he saw innocence and sweetness. The stubborn jut of her chin relaxed as she slept. She was a pretty woman, extremely pretty. But he preferred Carolyn when she was awake and full of fire.

He stood and gently lifted her from the floor. Though she shifted in his arms, she gave no sign of waking up. He placed her on the leather sofa and covered her with an afghan. Later he'd figure out a way to get her up to her own bed.

In moments he was dressed. He wished he had more time to stay with Carolyn. Spending the night in her arms would be sheer luxury.

But he had work to do.

In the dining room, he found Corelli hunched over his bank of computers. In spite of the hour, the only sign that Corelli was frazzled was the loosening of the knot on his necktie.

"Have you gotten any sleep?" Burke asked.

"Catnaps," Corelli replied. "I only require four hours a night."

Burke understood. He was much the same way. During the course of a job like this, he stayed pumped on adrenaline and coffee. Afterwards, he'd keel over and sleep for twenty-four hours. "What have you heard on the bug in Logan's office?"

"A lot," Corelli said. "If you want, I can play back every conversation."

"Give me a summary."

"The SOF mounted a search for Sunny. They have no clue that you were involved in her rescue, but Logan was quick to blame Carolyn. He said she was a bad influence who probably put the thought of running away in Sunny's mind. Then he called off the search. Their assumption is that she's here at the ranch."

Which validated what Carolyn had told him after

her phone conversation with Logan. Burke hadn't planned on taking Sunny to the hospital. But that move might have turned out to be a stroke of good fortune. "Tell me more."

"Apparently, there's discontent among the other women. Several of them—especially those with children—want out."

Burke would do his best to accommodate their wishes. If he could get the innocents away from Logan, there might be a chance to get inside the SOF and search for Nicole. "Any talk of the kidnapping?"

"Not a word," Corelli said. "The major topic of conversation is a big delivery. They're real careful not to say what it is. Even among themselves, they call it the Big D."

"A reference to whatever they're smuggling." Big D sounded like drugs, but the whole need for secrecy along a mountain pass and trail made him think of something larger. "I want you to interface with Logan's computer and find out more."

"Already done." Corelli permitted himself a grin. "Logan has been corresponding with other survivalist groups, similar to the Sons of Freedom."

"Meaning insignificant."

"Correct. These are small enclaves in remote areas of Texas, Arizona and Montana. None of them pop up on FBI surveillance records, but taken all together they form a network. My best guess is that they're smuggling illegal weaponry and drugs."

"Information that needs to be reported."

"Yes, sir," Corelli said.

An organized network of survivalists involved in smuggling was something the FBI—and several other government agencies—would be interested in. But Burke's main concern was Nicole's safety. "When the time is right, we'll pass this information along. For now. Our focus is the kidnap victim."

"Understood." Corelli looked toward a flashing light on his phone bank. "That's another call from Logan. Should I tell Carolyn or let it go to voice mail?"

"I'll take it," Burke said. He held the receiver to his ear and identified himself. "Special Agent J. D. Burke."

"I want Carolyn," Logan said.

I'll bet you do. "You can talk to me."

There was a moment of silence while Logan considered.

Burke had nothing to say to this ass. Logan had probably kidnapped Nicole. He'd definitely terrorized Sunny and threatened Carolyn. If he acted on that threat, if he so much as touched one hair on her head, Burke would rain terror on this self-important survivalist.

But that wasn't how he'd been taught as a negotiator. His job was to get Logan talking. He forced a conversational tone. "Let's talk, Logan. Why did you call?"

"I know you have Sunny at the ranch. I want her back."

Burke couldn't really use Sunny as a bargaining chip; there was no way he'd return the new mother and her baby to the SOF compound. But Burke did have something to offer. Logan was expecting a big shipment, and he wouldn't want the FBI around for that delivery.

"Here's the deal, Logan. My only concern is Nicole Carlisle's safety. If you help me find her, I'll pack up and go, taking the choppers and the searchers with me. You'll be left in peace."

"I want Sunny back."

Burke's jaw tightened. "She's not here."

"You're lying."

"Tell me about Nicole."

"Go to hell, Burke. I'm not scared of you or any of your fed buddies. And you can tell Carolyn that, too. Tell her that I'm holding her personally responsible for Sunny. She knows better than to cross me."

"Leave her out of this. You're talking to me now."

"Then let the consequences rest on your head."

"What consequences?"

"I will have my revenge."

He hung up before Burke could tell him what real revenge looked like. He pried his tense fingers from the telephone receiver and turned to Corelli. "When is the Big D supposed to happen?"

"Monday night."

The same night that the ransom was supposed to be delivered. A plan began to form in Burke's mind.

Chapter Sixteen

The next morning, Carolyn wakened to the full light of morning glaring around the edges of the closed shades in her bedroom. She glanced at the digital clock on her bedside table. Ten thirty-seven? She seldom slept this late.

The need to get moving warred with a contented lassitude—the aftermath of last night's incredible passion in the office. *How did I get into my bed?* She looked under the comforter and saw that she was wearing a pair of sweatpants and a T-shirt. *I don't remember getting dressed.*

But she did recall—in spectacular detail—making love to Special Agent J. D. Burke. A happy little sigh escaped her lips as she snuggled deeper under the comforter. A quiver rippled through her, a reminder of Burke's touch. She licked her lips, imagining that she could still taste him. Behind closed eyes, she saw his muscular chest and arms. His powerful body...

The door to her bedroom crashed open. Dylan charged toward her bed and shook her. "Carolyn, get up."

In an instant, she went from sweet reverie to full alert. "What is it?"

"Proof of life. We got a videotape. You need to see this."

She lunged from the bed and grabbed her plaid flannel bathrobe from the hook in the closet. Barefoot, she followed him down the stairs.

In the living room, she saw Corelli hooking up a dusty, old VCR player to the flat-screen television. In a crisp voice, he informed them that nobody used equipment like this anymore. Later, he'd transfer the images to a DVD. But they shouldn't hope for crystal-clear definition.

"Why not?" Polly demanded as she peeked over his shoulder.

"Twenty-first-century technology doesn't do me any good when the kidnapper is using stuff that's decades old. First, a Polaroid photograph. Then a pay phone. Now this."

Lucas was also in the room. And Special Agent Smith who, she assumed, had taken over the search coordination efforts since Silverman was at the hospital with Sunny.

Her gaze went to Burke. A forest-green turtleneck outlined his broad shoulders. Though his brown hair was mussed, he looked awake and supremely competent. His dark eyes met hers in brief acknowledgment. There was no time to indulge in morning-after conversation or sweet, sexy whispers. There could only be a glance between them.

Corelli pushed the play button and stepped away from the screen.

When Nicole's face appeared, Dylan shuddered.

"It's Sunday morning," Nicole said.

Behind her was a faded yellow sheet that looked like it had been tacked to a wall. The image showed only her head and shoulders. She reached up and tucked her blond hair behind her ear. "Don't worry about me," she said. "I'm fine. I have plenty to eat and drink, and I'm being well cared for."

Her blue eyes seemed calm and untroubled. Considering what she'd been through, she looked good.

"I've been asked to remind you about the ransom. One million dollars in cash. That's a lot of money, isn't it?" She drew her fingers across her lips. "If you follow instructions, everything will turn out okay. See you soon."

The screen went blank.

Burke moved in front of the screen. "First impressions?"

In a choked voice, Dylan spoke, "I've never seen that blouse before."

"Are you sure?" Carolyn asked. "I didn't think you paid much attention to clothes."

"I know what she had on yesterday. I'll never forget."

Polly said, "I think Dylan's right about the blouse. I've done my share of laundry here and Nicole doesn't have anything with flowers. I'm not so sure about the beige cardigan."

"First impressions," Burke repeated. "Carolyn?"

She forced her drowsy mind to focus. "It didn't sound like she was reading from a script. She was conversational, but distant. Like she was using her bedside manner."

"Explain," Burke said.

"I've gone with Nicole a couple of times when she's treating a sick animal. When she chats with the owner, she uses that tone."

"Right," Dylan said. "It's her 'Don't Panic' voice. She's trying to tell us to stay calm. Damn it, she always puts other people first."

"Lucas," Burke said, "what's your impression?"

"Didn't look like she'd been hurt none."

Carolyn studied the old, bowlegged cowboy. He sat on the edge of the sofa, leaning forward. His hair looked like it hadn't been washed recently, and his stubble was a couple of days old. More than anyone else in the room, he showed signs of falling apart. She wanted to believe it was because he was concerned about Nicole. But if he was the traitor, he'd feel guilty. Remorse would gnaw at his gut.

"Okay, Smith," Burke said. "Give us a profiler's opinion."

As Agent Smith stepped in front of the screen, Carolyn realized how short he was, probably only five feet seven inches, with square shoulders and a thick torso. His blond hair was cut short, military-style, and it made his head seem square.

"It's all good," he said. "As Lucas pointed out, she doesn't appear to be injured. Or drugged. The tone that Carolyn referred to as bedside manner might not only be for our benefit. She could have established a rapport with the kidnappers. That's positive."

"Why?" Dylan asked.

"In captivity, a hostage undergoes feelings of panic, fear and rage," he lectured. "Nicole appears to be suppressing those primal reactions. Instead, she's cooperating, forcing the kidnappers to see her as an individual, convincing them that she's on their side. In that circumstance, they're far less likely to hurt her."

As Burke paced across the floor, Carolyn couldn't help admiring the way he moved. Smooth, long strides. He said, "We're going to play this tape several times. I want you to look for any clue to her whereabouts. Nicole might be giving us some kind of signal."

"Like what?" Polly asked.

"A facial expression. The way she blinks. The way she phrases her words."

As she watched, again and again, Carolyn's anger returned. She wished she could jump inside the picture and drag Nicole home.

In the Polaroid, Nicole had put them on the right track with hand signals indicating the Circle M. This time, she seemed to be doing the same thing.

She had gestured twice. Once to tuck her hair behind her ear, forming a circle. Then she stroked her finger along the line of her mouth. Actually, three fingers. A sideways *M*.

Nicole's message was the same: Circle M.

Carolyn looked toward Lucas. If he was in communication with the SOF, she didn't want to say anything in front of him. He might report back and get Nicole in trouble. Why was Burke allowing Lucas to stay in the room?

"I'm drawing a blank," Polly said. "Anybody need coffee?"

Carolyn raised her hand. "I do."

Coffee and some kind of breakfast sounded heavenly. She followed Polly into the kitchen and poured herself a mug. "Thanks for moving up to the house, Polly. Did you sleep well?"

"I did, thank you. My husband could hardly close his eyes. He's so excited about being in the middle of all this. Not that he's happy about the kidnapping."

"Of course not." Carolyn understood that Polly's husband and his illness took precedence over anything else. "How long have you and Juan been married?"

"Almost twenty years. Second marriage for both of us." She grinned. "And the second time's the charm."

They had a good marriage, and Carolyn wondered what went into that kind of relationship. Was it something she could learn? "How did you know you and Juan were in love? Was it fast as lightning?"

"More like a slow, gathering storm. We were friends for months before anything happened. But as soon as he kissed me, I knew he was the man I'd spend the rest of my life with."

"All it took was one kiss?"

Polly raised an eyebrow. "You're asking a lot of questions, Carolyn. This wouldn't have anything to do with that good-looking FBI agent, would it?"

She wasn't ready to talk about Burke, not even to Polly. Carolyn sipped her coffee. "Where do you think Nicole got that blouse?"

"Not sure, but I was glad to see her in clean clothes." Polly opened the fridge and took out an orange. "You didn't answer my question about Burke."

"I guess I didn't."

"The way you were brought up, surrounded by cowboys and having to be as tough as they are, you need a man who's as strong-willed and stubborn as you. Burke would be a good match for you."

"That's your opinion," Carolyn said.

"Mark my words. You're not going to end up with some fancy-pants, city-boy lawyer."

Burke strode into the kitchen and they both went silent. He was definitely not a fancy-pants. The opposite, in fact. Totally rugged, he exploded with masculine energy.

"Get dressed, Carolyn. We're going for a ride on the Indian Trail."

"Give me fifteen minutes."

He checked his wristwatch, a habit that she'd come to realize was his way of maintaining control. "Ten," he said.

"Twelve," she countered.

"Meet me in the barn."

BURKE STOOD IN THE BARN doorway and tapped the face of his wristwatch. Twelve minutes had passed. He hadn't really expected Carolyn to get ready so quickly, and he was surprised to see her stride from the house wearing her boots, hat and a canvas jacket. From this distance, her expression was unreadable, but her confidence showed in every swaggering step she took.

Stopping in front of him, she planted her fists on her hips. "Fast enough for you?"

"You're a speed demon." He wanted to tell her that she was the sexiest demon he'd ever seen. Naturally beautiful. No need for makeup. Her black lashes and arched brows highlighted her transparent green eyes.

Carolyn took an energy bar from her jacket pocket and tore off the wrapping. "Mind telling me why I'm here?"

"I need your help to find the cave Sunny mentioned."

"Ah, yes. Her supposedly romantic hideaway near Cathedral Rocks." She raised the bar to her mouth. "I don't know the exact location, but I can take you to the rocks. Why are we going there?"

"It occurred to me that a secluded hideout might be the place where Nicole is being held, being guarded by Butch Thurgood and Richter. I was wrong about that."

"How do you know?"

"This morning, at first light, I sent the chopper team to investigate. They located the cave. No one was there."

"Then, why are we—"

"Closer inspection," he said. He nodded to two uniformed men who were already on horseback, waiting outside the corral. "These deputies are going to run some forensic tests. We might find evidence that Nicole was at the cave."

The search team in the chopper had also made another discovery. Hovering near the pine trees where Sunny met up with them last night, they spotted a grave-sized mound of earth. Tonight, under cover of darkness, he'd take a team to excavate.

Past experience taught him that the body would be buried at least two-and-a-half feet deep with rocks on top. Otherwise, the coyotes would have dug up the corpse of Barbara Ayers. A check of the FBI database showed that she and her sister, Lisa, were listed as missing persons. The sisters had disappeared over a year ago.

Carolyn chomped on the energy bar. "If we head out on the road, we'll hook up with the Indian Trail. It's easy to follow."

"I don't want to go that way," he said. "The SOF could be watching the ranch, and I don't want them to know what we're doing."

"Good point. We can go west, then south over the ridge. That way, we'll stay on Carlisle land for most of the ride."

"I knew you'd have an answer." He turned on his heel and went into the barn where their horses were saddled and ready. After Logan's threat of revenge, he hadn't really wanted Carolyn to leave the house. But he needed her help. "GPS isn't much good in unmarked mountain terrain."

She went directly to Elvis and stroked his nose. "We're going for a ride, pal. What do you think about that?"

Elvis bobbed his head. Burke had never seen a horse with so much personality. The bay with a white blaze on his forehead was one of a kind. Like his owner.

He went to a wood bench and picked up a Kevlar vest. "You need to wear this, Carolyn."

A frown pulled at the corner of her soft pink lips. "Why?"

"Because we need to take the SOF seriously." He lowered his voice, though no one else was in the barn. "Corelli accessed Logan's computer and he's been listening to the bug. Logan didn't see us make the rescue, but he assumes you're somehow responsible. He thinks you influenced Sunny."

"Of course he'd blame me. The wicked city woman."

"Put on the vest, Carolyn." He paused, then added the magic word. "Please."

She took the vest from him. "I don't see you wearing any kind of protection."

"Logan's ticked off at you, not me." She seemed to have that effect on people. "But I suppose you're right. I'll stop at the van and pick up my own vest."

"I don't want anything bad to happen to you."

"I'll be okay," he said. "Logan might have shot up my vehicle, but he's not dumb enough to injure a fed."

"Don't underestimate Sam Logan," she said. "He's a lot dumber than you think."

Chapter Seventeen

In spite of the uncomfortable bulletproof vest under her jacket, Carolyn was glad to take an active part in the investigation. Astride Elvis, she rode with Burke and the two deputies from the sheriff's department. They headed west toward the burned-out structure of the old stable. The acrid stench of charred wood hung like a poisonous cloud in the crisp air.

This was the first time she'd seen the destruction up close, and she reined Elvis in to take a closer look. The one-story structure had been reduced to a grotesque skeleton with only parts of walls still standing and rubble where there had once been neat stalls. A scorched backhoe—an expensive piece of equipment—huddled at the far edge of the stable like the remains of a prehistoric beast.

The fire had been her motivation for coming home, and the sight troubled her. Was Lucas responsible for this needless destruction? He'd admitted to being first on the scene. He was the one who called in the alarm. But she couldn't imagine him doing this, risking the livestock, risking a wildfire that could have spread across the grassland. They could have lost acres and acres. Lucas wouldn't want that; he loved this ranch. Or did he?

She didn't trust her own judgment anymore, not after seeing that list of enemies that Burke and his agents had compiled. Half the county seemed to hate the Carlisles.

Burke reined his big bay horse up beside her. She tore her gaze away from the ruins. Watching Burke was a welcome distraction. Despite the fact that he wore a Chicago Cubs cap instead of a Stetson, he looked comfortable in the saddle. Those summers he'd spent with his grandparents in rural Wisconsin had served him well. "You don't ride too badly," she said, "for a farmer."

"Once you learn how, you never forget."

But there seemed to be something else he'd entirely forgotten. He'd made no mention of their lovemaking. But then again, she hadn't said anything, either. *Should I tell him that he's the best lover I've ever known? That last night was spectacular?*

Though tempted to gush, she decided to play it cool. When she was younger, she'd had her share of meaningless sex and knew how it was supposed to work: no flowers, no phone calls in the morning, no sweet talk.

But last night was different. The depth of their passion wasn't what she expected from a one-night stand. Making love with Burke left her craving more. She didn't want last night to be the first and only time.

I should tell him. Instead, she nudged Elvis with her knees and moved forward. Skirting the edge of the forest, they came into sight of one of the main feeding pastures, about four miles from the ranch house. Contained by a barbed wire fence, over three hundred head of Black Angus milled from water troughs to feeding on the hay spread on the ground.

This was usually the last stop for these cattle before being herded to the slaughterhouse in Delta. Unlike non-organic ranches that crammed the cattle into feed lots and stuffed them with corn to fatten them up, this wide valley offered plenty of room to move around and graze.

Burke rode beside her. He pointed to a fat boulder near the south side of the field. "Interesting rock formation."

"*La Rana*," she said. "The frog. When I was a girl, I thought *La Rana* watched over the cattle at night and croaked really loud to chase away predators."

"A protector frog. Nice."

She regarded the herd with pride. "They're beautiful, aren't they?"

"Not the word that springs to mind when I think of a nine-hundred-pound steer."

"Don't you dare say fat." She bristled. "These guys are so healthy."

"When I think of beauty," he said, "I think of you."

Taken aback, she met his gaze. His dark brown eyes warmed her, melting her attempt to be cool. Without saying another word, he seemed to be telling her that last night had meant something more to him, too.

But they were busy people with full, active lives and tons of responsibility. She couldn't possibly think of settling down. Still, the idea of sharing her hectic life with Burke held a certain appeal. She imagined coming home after work and finding him waiting with a glass of Chardonnay. What would it be like to go on an actual date? Or to make love in an actual bed?

He urged his horse forward, leaving her gaping behind him. She took a moment to tamp down her fantasies, then tapped her heel against Elvis's flank. Her big brown horse happily sped up, bringing her even with Burke.

"About last night," she said, "I want you to know—"

"Not now," he interrupted.

His abrupt manner shouldn't have surprised her. By now she knew that Burke was a man whose action agenda easily outweighed his sensitivity. "Burke, I have something to say."

"So do I." The heat from his gaze poured over her like hot fudge on a sundae. "There's a hell of a lot to say, but now isn't the time. We need to keep focused on the kidnapping."

"Fine," she responded with as much gumption as she could dredge up while her insides liquefied into a gooey mass of desire. "Here's a point of focus. Why did you leave Lucas in the room when you played the tape of Nicole?"

"You think he's the traitor?"

She hadn't clearly stated her suspicion. Even now she was hesitant to accuse. "It's possible."

"You didn't want to say anything in front of him," Burke said. "That's why you didn't mention Nicole's hand gestures. She made another Circle M."

"Pointing at Logan. Again."

"I agree that Logan is probably our culprit," Burke said, "but there's something bothering me. We got ransom calls from two different kidnappers with requests for two different amounts. I have a nasty feeling that Butch and Richter might have taken Nicole and split off from the SOF to make their own big score."

"Any evidence?" she asked.

"Nothing. Corelli has been listening to the bug I placed in Logan's office nonstop. He hasn't mentioned Nicole once."

At this point, the trail went uphill through thick

forest and rocky terrain. They went single file with Carolyn in the lead. She hadn't been in this back-country for years, and the land had changed, as it always did. Rock formations stayed pretty much the same, but the forest was always different. During the last few years, they'd lost a lot of trees to pine beetles. Whole hillsides had to be clear-cut. Later, they'd be replanted.

She picked her route carefully, relying on an internal compass. Figuring out directions had always been easy for her. Her father once said that he could drop her in the middle of a forest at midnight and she'd find her way home by morning. Even with the sun almost directly overhead, she sensed that they were moving south and west.

If only life could be so easily navigated.

She paused at a high point on a ridge and waited for Burke and the deputies to ride up beside her. She pointed. "Over there. Do you see the sunlight hitting that jagged formation? Cathedral Rocks. That's where we're headed."

"Nice work," one of the deputies commented. "If I'd been leading the way, we would've been lost."

"When we get closer," Burke said, "it wouldn't hurt to be extra alert."

The two men nodded. One of them pulled his rifle from a scabbard attached to his saddle.

For the second time in as many days, Carolyn was on a mission with Burke where she was the only person without firepower. *Next time, I'll be armed.*

"You boys go first," Burke said. "I'll hang back with Carolyn."

As the deputies went around them, Carolyn gave a sharp tug on her horse's reins to hold him back. Elvis didn't like being in the rear.

The deputies in their brown uniform jackets rode carefully down a steep incline while Burke watched. Sitting straight in his saddle, he seemed suddenly alert. "This isn't your property anymore."

"It's National Forest."

He gave a nod. "You go first."

At the bottom of the craggy slope, they merged with the Indian Trail that led through the mountains. A dried-up creek bed sat on their left. On their right was a hillside of loose gravel. Compared to the narrow path they'd taken over the ridge, the Indian Trail was like a super highway with plenty of room to ride side by side.

"I can see why they'd use this route for smuggling," Burke said. "You could almost drive a truck through here."

"Not in the higher elevations. It's rugged. Crossing the pass isn't for sissies."

"When do you usually get snow around here?"

Supposedly, they couldn't mention last night because they needed to keep focus. But he was talking about the weather. The weather? She shot a ferocious glare in his direction and reined Elvis to a halt. "I refuse to go through a snowfall report. We need to talk about last night. About us."

"Not now." His gaze rested on her for a moment, then slid away. He was scanning the hillsides.

"What are you looking for?"

"Trouble," he said.

"Search no more. I'm sitting right here beside you. And I have a truckload of trouble to unload on your head." She paused for breath. "In the first place, I don't want you to think that I'm the kind of woman who tumbles into bed at a moment's notice."

"Why would I think that?"

She didn't stop to explain that she'd known him for only a day before they were making love on the floor in her brother's office. "Secondly, I don't expect any sort of commitment. I'm not looking to get married or anything."

"Carolyn, I don't—"

"Furthermore," she said, "last night was amazing. We have some kind of connection. I can't explain it."

"Then don't." He maneuvered his horse beside her and held out his hand. "Lean over here and kiss me."

"As if that will make everything all right?"

"You know it will."

She reached toward his hand. Before she could grasp it, he turned his head sharply. "Carolyn, get down."

She heard the gunfire. Then a thud.

She was hit.

Her breath was gone. It felt like all the air had been squeezed out of her lungs. *Breathe, damn it.* She gulped frantically but couldn't get air. She was losing consciousness. She slumped. Her feet came out of the stirrups. Falling, falling…

Burke was there. He caught her before she hit the ground. Ducking behind Elvis, he cradled her against him.

A throbbing pain spread from her chest to every part of her body. She'd been shot. If she hadn't been wearing the bulletproof vest, she'd be dead.

She sucked down a gasp of air, then another. Her arms and legs regained strength, but she wasn't able to stand on her own.

Burke yelled to the deputies. "Sniper. In the trees. Straight ahead."

Dazed, she leaned against him as he used his cell phone to summon the chopper. Using Elvis as a shield, he dragged her to the edge of the trail. Behind a boulder, they found shelter.

Her pain began to subside. Pressed against the rock, she looked up at him.

He had saved her life.

Chapter Eighteen

Burke held Carolyn close, protecting her with his body in case there was another shooter behind them. He pulled off his Cubs cap and rose up to look over the flat boulder where they were hiding. In his right hand, he held his gun, ready to return fire. He couldn't attack. There was no effective way to aim at the sniper perched on the hillside and keep Carolyn safe at the same time.

He knew where the shooter was. At the moment he'd been leaning toward Carolyn for a kiss, he'd caught a glimpse in his peripheral vision: the sharp reflection of sunlight on a rifle scope. But he'd been too late to do anything more than shout a warning.

Farther up the trail, the deputies returned fire. He hoped they could keep the sniper pinned down until the chopper arrived.

Carolyn moved in his arms. "Where's Elvis? And your horse?"

Burke looked over his shoulder. Both horses were gone. He didn't see the mounts the deputies had been riding. "They took off. They're safe."

"Let me up, Burke. I'm okay. I just had the wind knocked out of me."

He held her even tighter. Their Kevlar vests bumped against each other. "The chopper's going to be here in a minute."

"I can handle this. I'm okay."

He looked down into her anxious face. "Lie still and let me keep you safe. You don't have to prove anything to me."

Her green eyes flashed. "You're right. The only person I have to prove anything to…is me. I never thought of it that way before, but it's true."

He wasn't sure what she was talking about, but he was glad to hear her speaking. When she toppled from her horse and he thought she'd been seriously wounded, his world stopped. She'd almost gotten killed, and it was his fault. "I never should have put you in danger."

"You saved my life," she said. "If I hadn't been wearing this vest, I'd be dead."

"I shouldn't have brought you here."

After last night, when she'd been so effective in rescuing Sunny, he'd made the mistake of thinking that she was as experienced as Smith or Silverman. Using her as a guide through the mountains broke FBI protocol. She was a civilian, someone who shouldn't be placed in the line of fire.

She wriggled her arm free and touched the place on the vest where she'd been hit. "I was shot. I'm going to have a giant bruise. Otherwise, I'm fine. It's kind of amazing really."

"You're amazing," he said.

An exchange of gunfire between the deputies and the sniper distracted him. He peeked over the edge of the boulder they were hiding behind. The two deputies seemed to be doing a good job.

"Logan must really hate me," she said. "Do you think he's the sniper?"

"Is he a good shot?"

"Not really. He probably sent one of his men to do his dirty work."

He lay back down beside her, aware of the possibility that another of Logan's men had moved into position behind them. At any given moment, Burke could be shot in the back, and he didn't want to die—didn't want to go until he told her. "About last night..."

"Now you're ready to talk?"

"Here's how I feel. You said you wanted me to know you're not a bimbo who sleeps around. The thought never entered my mind. You're a smart, principled woman. Different from anyone—male or female—that I've ever known. Maybe that's why I'm drawn to you. I can't figure you out. You challenge me in a good way. And I want to be with you. You can call that a bond or kismet or fate. I don't know what it is. I'm not one for analyzing. I just know it's there. It's real."

A tear slipped down her cheek.

Gently, he wiped it away. "You said you weren't ready to get married. You're probably right about that. It might be too soon. But I want you to know that I'm not afraid of commitment."

"I'm not afraid, either," she said.

Pressed against the boulder, they held each other. Her legs twined with his. In the midst of danger, he felt at peace. He'd rather be here with Carolyn than anywhere else.

He heard the *thunk-thunk* of the helicopter rotors and looked up.

The chopper couldn't land in this canyon, but the hovering bird made an effective predator as it swooped down. There was more gunfire. More shouts from the deputies. A bullhorn voice from the chopper shouted an order to put down the weapon and raise both hands.

Carolyn looked up at him. "What's happening?"

"We're being rescued."

He rose to a crouch and peeked over the boulder.

The deputies were waving their arms. Coming toward Burke and Carolyn, they called out, "They got him."

Burke stood. On the far hillside, he saw a man

standing with his arms raised over his head. Even at this distance, he knew it wasn't Logan; he wasn't blond.

One man from the chopper aimed a rifle at their quarry. Another descended on a rope to make the arrest. Impressive work.

Carolyn stood and leaned against his chest.

They were safe. For now.

TWO HOURS LATER, Carolyn had been evacuated from the Indian Trail. Elvis and all the other horses were safely tucked away in the stable. She'd been checked by a medic who told her that she was okay, apart from a bad bruise above her right breast. The medic gave her pain meds and suggested she go back to bed. Though she'd taken his advice, she couldn't sleep. Her mind whirled, remembering what had happened and trying to imagine what would come next.

She couldn't stop thinking about Burke. Instead of wondering whether or not he felt anything for her, she accepted him at his word. They had something special. And it might lead to a commitment between them. Joyful warmth flowed through her veins and she immediately felt guilty.

Nicole was still in danger. Jesse Longbridge was still unconscious in the hospital. The Carlisle Ranch was under siege. Not to mention the fact that Logan wanted her dead. In the middle of this disaster, how could she be happy?

She threw off the covers, climbed out of bed and got dressed. The pain medications were making her dizzy, and her bruise still throbbed, but she had to do something. It wasn't in her nature to lie back and let someone else take responsibility.

Completely dressed except for her boots, she heard a tap on her door. "Come in. I'm decent."

Burke stepped through her bedroom door and closed it behind him. His smile sparked those irrelevant happy feelings that she'd almost squelched.

"Too bad you're decent," he said. "I was hoping for a sexy lace negligee."

"Not at the ranch." She couldn't help smiling back. "All my classy nightwear is at my condo in Denver."

"Can't wait to see it."

He lived in Denver, too. That was his full-time residence when he wasn't on assignment. "What part of town do you live in?"

"I've got a duplex in Capitol Hill. You?"

"A condo. Twelfth floor. Downtown."

They lived less than five miles apart. They probably went to the same restaurants, shopped at the same stores, walked past each other on the street. But they had to come all the way to Carlisle Ranch to meet.

He sat on a burgundy upholstered chair beside her trophy case. "I wanted to give you an update."

She'd been thinking about something far more

sensual, but Burke had gone into his get-things-done mode. Instead of stretching out on the bed, she perched on a chair opposite him and shoved her feet into her boots. "I'm ready."

"The sniper's name is Wesley Tindall. He's former military—and that's where he learned to shoot. We're holding him in FBI custody."

She touched the bruise below her shoulder. "Was he the guy who shot out the window of your van?"

"Don't know. He's not talking. Hasn't said anything about Nicole, either."

"So, basically, he's not much use."

"Except that he won't be riding with Logan when they go to pick up their big shipment. He's down a man. And that's good news for us."

"Why?"

"On Monday night, when Logan and his men go to pick up the shipment, they'll leave the Circle M with fewer guards than usual. That's when we'll make our move. We'll go in, get the women and children out. And search for Nicole."

She liked the way that sounded. If Sunny was any indication, there would be plenty of other women who were ready to leave the SOF. "I want to be a part of that action."

"No."

"But some of the women know me. I can talk to them."

"This isn't up for negotiation." He stood. "I

almost lost you today. I won't put you in danger again."

She rose from her chair to face him. "That's my choice."

"I'm in charge here, Carolyn. It's my job."

But she didn't want to sit on the sidelines. "I'll be careful."

"We were careful today," he reminded her. "We went the long way around to avoid being seen."

Which brought up a question she hadn't considered before. "Why was Tindall there?"

"It wasn't an ambush," Burke said. "If Logan had been planning to trap us, there would have been more men. I think Tindall was posted as a lookout on the Indian Trail. It was our bad luck to run into him."

"Why did he shoot?"

"My guess? Logan has put out a bounty on you. He wants revenge. That's a damn good reason why you're not going to be involved in any more action."

"You make a good argument," she conceded. "But I still think I could—"

"No." He closed the distance between them in three quick strides. Reaching out, he caressed her shoulder. His hand came to rest behind her neck, and he held her so she couldn't look away from him. "Today, when I thought I'd lost you, my heart broke. If anything happened to you, I couldn't live with myself."

His tone struck a chord within her. "If I'm not there at your side," she said, "who's going to protect you?"

"I'll manage."

He kissed her hard, silencing her objections. Her body fit perfectly with his. Every contour matched. In his arms, she felt soft and feminine.

Just as quickly as he'd kissed her, he stepped back. "I wasn't planning to do that."

"I don't mind." She rested the flat of her palm against his solid, muscular chest. "Not a bit."

He caught her hand, brushed his lips against her knuckles. "There's more."

"I'm listening." She flopped on the bed, wishing that she was wearing a sexy negligee instead of jeans and boots.

"The sheriff's deputies finally got to do a forensic workup inside the cave. They found some fibers that look like they'd purposely been pulled from a sweater. The color matches the sweater Nicole was wearing when she was kidnapped."

"She was at the cave," Carolyn said. "Leaving us another clue."

"Here's the timeline I've got figured out," he said. "Nicole was grabbed at the creek by two guys associated with the SOF. They took her to the Circle M. Logan must have realized that there was a search underway."

"Right," she said, "my brother and his posse going door-to-door and asking questions."

"They had to get her out of there. Logan's men—Butch Thurgood and Pete Richter—took her to the cave, planning to wait until the search died down. The next day or late that night, he knew the FBI was involved. There'd be choppers and surveillance. The cave wasn't safe."

"So he had her brought back to the SOF compound," she said. "That's why Nicole keeps giving us Circle M clues."

Though he nodded, he didn't look convinced. It seemed like a lot of shuffling around. "Another alternative is that Butch and Richter took off with her. That would explain the second ransom call. They're trying to work their own angle."

She frowned. "If Nicole isn't at the Circle M, why would she give these clues and why *wouldn't* Logan let us search?"

"Because the place is loaded with illegal weapons and drugs. He can't allow an FBI search."

Carolyn wasn't sure if she preferred thinking of Nicole being with Logan or with his men. From what Sunny had told them, Pete Richter was mean.

"Tonight," Burke said, "we're going to excavate the grave site Sunny told us about. Chopper surveillance found a mound of earth near the pines."

This time, Carolyn didn't ask if she could come along. Digging up the remains of Barbara Ayers wasn't a mission she wanted to be part of. "Be careful, Burke."

Chapter Nineteen

The wind blew colder tonight. Heavy clouds scrolled across the face of the moon. Burke moved into position at the open field across from the pine trees where they'd met Sunny. He had a small army—Agent Smith and four other men called in for tactical support. Fully equipped, they were dressed like a SWAT team with weapons, full body armor and infrared goggles.

Their goal was to excavate Barbara Ayers's grave and recover her body. Her remains would be transported to the FBI medical examiner's office in Denver where a top-notch forensic team would read the evidence left behind in death—evidence that would lay the murder of this young, pregnant woman at the doorstep of Sam Logan and the SOF.

Furthermore, tonight was a practice run for tomorrow. Burke's men had studied the maps of the compound, but there was nothing like firsthand experience to get the lay of the land.

Tomorrow, while most of the SOF men were gone—dealing with their shipment on the Indian Trail—Burke and his force would penetrate the compound and extract the fourteen women and children. When these hostages were safe, he'd search for Nicole.

That rescue—less than twenty-four hours from right now—would take place at the same time Logan's men were meeting their contacts on the Indian Trail. At that location, he expected immediate surrender to a far superior force. There was nothing like a half dozen armed FBI agents and a chopper bearing down like a fierce, prehistoric beast to make a guy throw down his gun and beg for mercy.

At his signal, his men moved across the open field. The heat-sensing camera showed no guards in this area outside the barbed wire surrounding the compound.

They found the mound of earth that had been spotted by the chopper easily. Burke and Smith stood watch while the others dug. In less than five minutes, they had uncovered the remains of a small woman wrapped in a sheet.

They zipped her into a body bag, and spent another five minutes replacing the dirt.

They retreated across the field to the waiting vans.

The operation went off without a single hitch.

Apparently, Logan had more to worry about than guarding the grave of a woman who had been under his care.

CAROLYN PACED IN HER BEDROOM, waiting for Burke to return. It was only ten o'clock but felt much later. After being cooped up in the house all afternoon, she yearned for action. But she had promised not to take any risks, which included standing at her bedroom window with the light behind her back, going onto the well-lit porch or—Heaven forbid!—going to the barn for a chat with Elvis.

She touched the injury on her chest as a reminder that she was a target. Her bruise had turned a dark, aching purple and her arm was sore, but otherwise she was fine.

Her pacing stopped in front of the trophy case, filled with dozens of blue ribbons and gold statuettes that she'd started collecting when she was eight. Life had been simple then. All she had to do was go to school, finish her chores and ride.

Perhaps it was childish to keep the glass-and-wood trophy case in her room, but her father had built it with his own hands and presented it to her on her sixteenth birthday. He'd told her that she was a winner, and she'd worked her hardest to prove him right. She hadn't displayed any of her second- or third-place awards because she needed to be number one—to make her father proud. *The ultimate daddy's girl. But what choice did I have after Mom left?*

Carolyn realized that she still hadn't told her mother about the kidnapping. She needed to do that, but ten o'clock in Colorado was midnight in New York. Too late to call?

But this was important—one of the few times in her life when she needed her mother's advice. Not only about the kidnapping. She wanted to talk about Burke. Her feelings for him were a jagged chart of highs and lows. The way he needed to always be in charge—their constant competition—irked her. But when he touched her, she soared to a high that was unlike anything she'd felt before. Was it love?

She needed her mother, and she needed to make that very private call on a phone that wasn't tied to the system being monitored by Corelli.

Leaving her bedroom, she went downstairs. In the dining room, Corelli—who never seemed to sleep—was still monitoring his computers. Dylan had zonked out in the easy chair. She didn't want to wake her brother by talking to Corelli. Nor did she want Dylan to know that she was calling Mom.

Instead, she went through the kitchen and out the back door where she sat on the step. With the Longbridge Security men and other patrolling cowboys around, she felt safe.

The night chill soothed her. Finally, the weather was beginning to feel more like December. She zipped up her sweatshirt. When this ordeal was over, she'd need a vacation. Maybe she should spend Christmas in New York with Mom. All the decorated store windows were spectacular, and she'd love to see the giant tree in Rockefeller Center. Maybe Burke would come with her. They could get a room in a plush hotel, eat fabulous sushi or take in a play. Would he like theater? He'd been a cop in Chicago. He must be okay with big cities.

She spotted someone heading toward the house. Even in the dim light of the cloud-covered moon, she recognized the bowlegged gait of Lucas Mann.

She waved to him, and he ambled toward her.

"It's late," she said. "What are you doing awake?"

"Can't sleep. That's one of them things about being an old codger. You get up during the night."

She didn't want to think he was sleepless because he was haunted by guilt or that he was awake because he was spying for Logan. "Do you ever think about retirement? Buying a little spread of your own?"

"Matter of fact, I do. A quiet spot with a couple of horses."

Had Logan bribed him? Offered him enough cash to make his dream come true? "We'd hate to lose you."

"A man gets old." His eyes were shaded and unreadable under his cowboy hat. "You know how people talk about a slippery slope? How you take one wrong step and the whole mountain slides out from under you?"

What wrong step had he taken? "Is there something you need to tell me?"

With a gloved hand, he patted her shoulder. "Don't you worry none. Nicole's coming back. Then everything's going to get back to normal."

"I hope so."

He touched the brim of his hat and walked away. She cared about this old cowboy. He was like part of the family. But if he'd been involved in Nicole's kidnapping, in any way, she could never forgive him.

Before she could make her call, she heard vans pulling up at the front of the house. Burke was back. She rushed inside just as he came through the front door. In his full body armor, he was as impressive as an ancient warrior.

"It's done," he said.

"You found the body?"

He gave a somber nod.

In the back of her mind, she'd been hoping that the grave would be empty. Now there was evidence. One of the men in the SOF was a killer. That didn't bode well for Nicole.

She watched and listened while Burke debriefed

Corelli and Dylan. At the same time, he peeled off his armor and returned to the shape of a mere mortal—a shape she found incredibly attractive.

They moved on to discuss other plans. Tomorrow night was when everything was going down. In less than twenty-four hours, the ransom was due. And the SOF would be accepting their big delivery.

Neither Carolyn nor Dylan would participate in the hostage rescue. Their job was to stay here by the phone, waiting for the kidnappers to call.

The tactical support team circled the table. None of these men asked for her opinion, much less her approval of their plan. She'd become a tiny, insignificant speck of female energy, silently worrying that someone would be hurt, fearing for the safety of Nicole and the other SOF women. She remembered Lisa Ayers's sad eyes. How would that delicate, waiflike creature deal with all of these rescuers? And what about Nicole, being held against her will? Carolyn wished with all her heart that there was another way to deal with the situation, but she knew Logan would never negotiate.

She stepped away from the table. "Good night, boys. I'm going to bed."

"That's the right idea," Burke said. "We need to be rested. It's all going down tomorrow night."

A deep rumble of masculine voices echoed his words. These were men at the edge of battle, fierce and determined. Unstoppable.

She'd barely gotten into her bedroom when Burke slipped through the door. He caught hold of her hand and yanked her into his arms. His lips were hot. Her body responded to his urgent need as she kissed him back and drew his tongue into her mouth. His hands slid under her sweatshirt. His touch against her bare skin set off a chain reaction of desire.

And yet she pulled away from him. "Wait a minute."

"Am I being too rough? Did I hurt your bruise?"

"I'm not in pain," she assured him. "I just wanted to have a say in what happens next."

He reached up and ran his fingers through her unbound hair. "Soft as silk," he murmured.

She'd had time today for washing and conditioning, even though it was difficult with her aching left arm.

"Burke," she snapped. "Pay attention."

"I'm listening."

All she wanted was to be heard. "Your tactical support team is even more overpowering than a roomful of cowboys."

"Adrenaline," he said. "Our mission went off with precision. It's a satisfying feeling, even though we were dealing with the tragedy of a murder."

"I felt invisible, and I hate that. It's not normal for me. I'm accustomed to being in charge."

"I'll make you a deal, Carolyn. In this room, you're the boss. I'll do anything you want."

His pseudonegotiation made her smile. "What if I tell you to hop on one leg and squawk like a chicken?"

"That's a little kinky." He leaned close and nipped at her earlobe. "But I'll do it. Whatever turns you on."

Her need for control was overwhelmed by a more powerful desire. She placed her cell phone on the bedside table. The call to her mom would have to wait.

"I want you in my bed. All night."

"Yes, ma'am."

THE NEXT MORNING started much like the day before, except with fewer doubts. Carolyn glowed with a pleasant certainty. Burke was the best, most skillful lover she'd ever known. His passion took her to sensual places she'd never been before.

For the moment, she didn't mind not being the boss. She'd gotten out of bed, dressed and readied herself for the big day when the ransom would be paid and Nicole returned.

In the kitchen, she was sipping Polly's excellent coffee and had almost finished a plate of scrambled eggs and toast when Dylan joined her.

"We got another tape," he said.

"Where did it come from?"

"Just like yesterday, it was hanging on a fence post near the road. Whoever is dropping these tapes off is doing it before dawn and disappearing. Corelli says there's no point in checking satellite surveillance. The mountains and trees make it impossible to identify the guy."

Taking her coffee, she followed him into the living room where Burke stood by the television. The sight of his big, muscular body gave her a warm feeling of possessiveness. *My man. He's my man.* And she wouldn't trade him in for a multimillion-dollar distribution contract.

Corelli pushed a button, and Nicole's image appeared on the television screen. She was wearing a different blouse—cotton with blue flowers. The same faded sheet hung behind her.

"Monday morning," she said. "It's getting close to Christmas. I miss doing the decorating."

As she reached up and pushed her hair off her face, Carolyn noticed two things. This gesture wasn't any sort of clue. And Nicole was wearing her wedding band on the wrong hand. This wasn't a trick of videotape reversal. Carolyn knew the ring was on Nicole's right hand because she wore her wristwatch on her right wrist.

"Anyway," Nicole said, "I want to say that I'm sorry. I'm sorry for everything that's happened. Still, there might be a silver lining. I'm always an optimist. Right, Dylan? Maybe this is all for the best."

When the screen went blank, Carolyn felt an

ominous chill. There was something very different about Nicole. She looked the same as yesterday— clean and healthy. But her attitude had changed. And why change her wedding ring to her right hand? It was almost like she didn't want to be married anymore.

"All for the best," Carolyn repeated Nicole's words. "What does that mean?"

Dylan's face was pale. His hands drew into fists. "She's an optimist. Always thinks things are going to be great, even when the odds are against it."

Was he talking about Nicole's desire to have a baby? The struggle they'd gone through trying to get pregnant? "What does that mean to you?"

"You know me, sis. I always look for problems, trying to anticipate what might go wrong."

"It sounds like Nicole is telling you to have hope. Tonight, we'll pay the ransom. She'll be back here where she belongs, hanging Christmas decorations and wrapping presents."

"Maybe," he conceded. "But we still haven't gotten a call from the kidnappers telling us where to deliver the ransom. We still don't know where and how Nicole will be released. I see the glass as half-empty."

A lot could go wrong. They all knew it.

The trick was to make it through today into tonight. The long hours stretched in front of her like an eternity.

Carolyn went into the dining room and grabbed a cell phone that wasn't connected to anything else. She pressed in a number that she knew by heart.

When the phone was answered, Carolyn spoke four words that she'd never said before: "Mom? I need you."

Chapter Twenty

Burke hardly recognized Corelli without his tie and suit jacket. Wearing a bulletproof vest and a heavy jacket to ward off the night chill, the computer expert had positioned himself behind a bank of computer screens inside an FBI van. His job for the assault on the SOF compound would be communications.

Burke squatted beside him, cramped by the small space inside the van. "You know, Corelli, I'm still not sure you should leave the ranch house."

"I trained Dylan on how to work the phones. He's a smart guy. He can handle it." For proof, Corelli touched a button on one of the monitors. "Dylan? How's everything at the house?"

"Quiet." The answer came through, loud and clear.

"Is Carolyn there?" Burke asked.

"Hi, Burke. What's up?"

The sound of her voice made him want to turn

around and go back to the ranch. He didn't like leaving her and Dylan there with only the cowboys and Sheriff Trainer for protection.

"We're waiting," he said. "It sounds like Logan and his boys are planning their meet on the Indian Trail any minute."

At this time of year, sundown came early. Right now, it was almost dark.

"We're waiting, too," she said. "For the ransom delivery call. Corelli is going to keep us posted, right?"

"Right," Burke said. "The same goes for you and Dylan. Let us know about any calls."

"Burke." She spoke his name softly. "Be careful. Please."

"Back at you."

He didn't repeat his warning that neither she nor her brother should leave the ranch house to deliver the ransom until he'd returned. He'd said those words so many times today that they should be permanently etched on that highly intelligent brain of hers.

She knew the risks. More importantly, she understood that a coordinated ransom delivery had a far greater likelihood of success than a half-baked effort from her and her brother.

Bottom line, he hoped the ransom would never need to be paid. Once his force got inside the SOF compound and searched, he hoped to find Nicole.

At this point, that hope was paper-thin. Though Nicole had twice signaled them that she was at the Circle M and Burke was relatively sure that Logan made the second ransom call to Carolyn's phone, the kidnapping hadn't been mentioned on the bug in Logan's trailer office or in any e-mail correspondence.

"They're on the move," Corelli said.

Earlier today, three heat-sensing cameras had been placed at strategic locations to monitor activity inside the compound. One focused on the front gate. Another showed the western route that Burke and his men would use to enter the Circle M. A far-range scope showed the compound buildings, including Logan's trailer and the bunkhouse where the women and children spent most of their time.

Like the bugs and computers, these cameras showed no clue about Nicole's whereabouts. She might be mingled with the other women. *Or she might be somewhere else entirely.*

"Two trucks," Corelli said. "Driving toward the front gate."

The greatest threat to their rescue operation came from Logan's surveillance cameras. Very likely, he'd leave a man behind to monitor those cameras, which would show the approach of Burke and the seven men working with him.

The first order of business—Burke's job—was

to pin down the man in the trailer so he couldn't interfere with the hostage rescue.

"Three men in each truck," Corelli said.

Burke did the math. Logan had told him there were thirteen men, counting himself. Tindall the sniper was already in custody. That made twelve.

In his surveillance, Corelli had only seen ten. Either Logan had a couple of defections or the notorious twosome of Thurgood and Richter weren't on the compound. They could be somewhere else, holding Nicole.

Even though storming the SOF compound might not bring Nicole back, there were other reasons to close Logan down: the murder of Barbara Ayers and the smuggling network.

Burke returned his focus to the screens in front of Corelli. There were thirteen men less Tindall, Thurgood, Richter and the six men in the trucks. "Only four men left at the Circle M," Burke said.

"Two at the gate. Two in the trailer, monitoring their surveillance cameras." Corelli gave a short laugh. "They're watching us watch them."

"Not for long."

Burke climbed out of the van and stretched. Even in body armor, he knew that he wasn't invincible, but he liked his odds for getting through this operation without injury. He had seven men in body armor to deal with four cowboys.

He activated the microphone that allowed him to communicate with the rest of his team. "Let's do it."

WITH SHERIFF TRAINER and two deputies keeping watch on the porch, Carolyn was alone with her brother in the dining room. He'd taken Corelli's position behind the computer monitors.

After all the activity of the past few days, it seemed strangely quiet. She drummed her fingers on the tabletop. Might as well tell Dylan now and get it over with. "I talked to Mom."

"Why?"

"Because this is a time when we need to reach out to family. She'll be here tomorrow around noon."

His forehead puckered as he frowned. Dylan had a lot more issues with their mother than she did. "I can't believe she agreed to come back to the ranch. When she left us, she couldn't get away from here fast enough."

"She came back for your wedding," Carolyn reminded him.

"And she gave us a very nice gift. And Nicole wrote her a very nice thank-you card. That's that."

She didn't mention her opinion that their father hadn't been the easiest man in the world to live with. The portrait of their father, Sterling Carlisle, as a rough and rugged rancher who was building an empire and not paying much attention to his family might also apply to Dylan.

In the videotape, Nicole had been wearing her wedding ring on the wrong hand. That worried Carolyn. She feared that the problems between Dylan and his wife ran deeper than a single issue, and she hated to see their family history repeat in another broken marriage.

Were the Carlisles incapable of handling long-term relationships? She rose from the table and paced. She and Burke weren't at the point where they were planning beyond tomorrow, but making a commitment didn't scare her. And Burke was, as he'd said himself, afraid of nothing.

Suddenly, Dylan scrambled with the phones. "It's the kidnapper. I recognize the phone number."

"I'll take the call," she said. "You record it and start the trace."

He nodded.

Carolyn tried not to show fear. "This is Carolyn."

"It's time," said the whispery voice on speaker-phone. "Bring the ransom to *La Rana*."

Her instructions were to keep him talking. "That's a big pasture. I'm not exactly sure where you want me to put it."

"On the rocks. Go. Now."

"It's going to take a while to get saddled up and—"

"He hung up," Dylan said.

Burke's warning echoed in her head. He'd told them not to leave the house until he got back.

"Damn it," Dylan said. "He's calling back."

He put the call through. This time the voice was Nicole's. "Dylan, are you there?"

"Yes," he said. "Where are you?"

"Meet me at the creek in half an hour. After the ransom is dropped off."

"Are you all right?"

"Just be there."

The phone went dead.

As soon as Burke and Smith were on Circle M land and within range of the surveillance cameras, they started running. A full-out sprint in body armor while carrying a heavy-duty repeating rifle wasn't easy, but his adrenaline surged. Burke was flying.

He went first, since he'd actually been inside the compound and knew the layout of the buildings. The barn was in sight. He ran toward the trailer. His plan was to keep the men inside pinned down, unable to interfere in the rescue of the women and children.

Through his headset, he heard Corelli's voice. "Keep going. They're moving inside. Haven't left the trailer yet."

Burke and Smith split up. Smith ducked behind a Jeep parked to the left of the trailer door. Burke ran to the left side. He called out, "FBI. Throw down your weapons. Come out with your hands up."

The response was a blast of bullets fired through the door. If Burke had been dumb enough to stand there, he would have been mowed down.

Both he and Smith let loose with a barrage of gunfire. As agreed, they aimed low, almost into the dirt. Burke didn't want casualties. He circled the trailer, staying away from the windows.

From the bunkhouse, he heard shouts of protest.

The corresponding voices of his men, heard through his headset, were polite. They explained that they were there to protect the women and children, to remove them from a dangerous situation.

In just a few minutes, the head of the rescue team reported, "We're leaving with the hostages. Three men are escorting them. Two more are headed back toward the guys at the front gate."

The plan seemed to be operating smoothly, and that concerned Burke. After years in law enforcement, he knew that nothing was easy.

He spotted a woman running toward the trailer. One who had broken away from the others?

She screamed, "Logan, look out! They're coming for you, Logan!"

A shot was fired. *From inside the trailer.*

The woman fell.

DYLAN REFUSED TO WAIT. Nicole's phone call had raised his level of anxiety to a fever pitch. "We're going to deliver that damn ransom. And we're going to do it right now."

"Use your head, Dylan. It's a trick. The kidnappers have to be watching the house. They know we're alone. If we wait until Burke gets back…"

"Nicole could be dead by then."

Carolyn begged him. "Please. Let's call Burke."

"That was my wife on the phone. She wouldn't lie to me."

She might not have a choice. The kidnappers could be standing over her with a gun. "I heard her."

"She said to meet her in half an hour. After we pay the ransom." He held Carolyn's shoulders and looked into her eyes. In his face, she saw the depth of his suffering. "Either you help me with this or I'll do it alone."

How could she refuse her brother? She'd promised her father that she'd protect him. And he had a point. If they didn't deliver the ransom, Nicole might pay the ultimate price.

"I'll ride with you," she said.

"Not enough time. *La Rana* and the creek are in opposite directions. We'll never make it to both in half an hour."

He was correct, and the timing was important. She drew the obvious conclusion. "There must be two of them. One to pick up the ransom. The other to hold Nicole."

"Butch Thurgood and Pete Richter." He stormed from the dining room and grabbed his jacket near the door. "Bastards."

"I'll drop the ransom at *La Rana*," she said. "You go and wait for Nicole."

"I'll grab a couple of horses from the men and bring them to the back door. Hurry."

"What are you going to tell the sheriff?"

"I'll figure it out." He wrapped his arms around her for a quick hug. "Thanks, sis. I love you."

"Love you, too. Be careful."

While he went to make explanations and find them a couple of mounts, she entered the office to retrieve the ransom from the safe.

Her fingers trembled as she spun the dial on the combination lock and took out the heavy backpack. This might be the biggest mistake she'd ever made. Remembering the fierce blast to her chest when she'd been shot, she wished that she had one of those uncomfortable bulletproof vests.

She put on her jacket and jammed her arms into the straps of the backpack. No time to waste.

Still, she returned to the computers in the dining room and activated the channel Dylan had used to communicate with Corelli. "I have a message for Burke."

"Carolyn?"

"I'm delivering the ransom now."

"Wait," Corelli said. "Don't make a move until—"

"Tell him *La Rana*."

She turned off the channel and ran for the door, trying to outrace her better judgment.

Chapter Twenty-One

Burke watched the woman writhing on the ground, holding her leg and crying. He couldn't leave her there, suffering. But he couldn't rescue her without stepping directly into the line of fire. The man inside that trailer had been cold-blooded enough to shoot someone who was trying to warn him.

It had to be Logan.

"Logan," Burke yelled. "This is your last chance to disarm and come out with your hands up."

"Then what? Prison?" It was Logan, all right. "Get off my land, fed."

Burke would have preferred waiting until his teams had the women and children safely loaded into transport. He heard gunfire and shouting from the front gate where another confrontation was underway.

He spoke into his microphone, "Give me a report on the hostages."

"One woman ran off. We're almost to the vehicles with the others."

"Move fast," Burke said. He didn't know what else Logan might have up his sleeve.

Another voice came through the headset. "We're at the front gate. Both men have surrendered."

The only problem left was Logan, holed up in his trailer.

Burke wanted this over. He wanted to get back to the ranch and to Carolyn. The thought of her spurred him on.

He stepped away from the trailer. From his belt, he unclipped a flashbang canister—similar to a grenade but without the lethal effects. This canister would make a big noise and a fierce burst of blinding white light before exuding a stinging burst of smoke. Should be enough to drive the rattle-snake from his hole.

Aiming high, Burke shot out a side window on the trailer and lobbed the canister inside.

He turned his head aside so he wouldn't be affected by the flash. The blast was deafening. Smoke poured through the broken window.

From inside the trailer came yelps of surprise.

Burke moved into position near the bullet-riddled trailer door. He saw Agent Smith emerge from his hiding place behind the vehicle and position himself in front of the injured woman so she wouldn't be caught in the crossfire. Smith would take care of her.

Logan flung open the door. His heavy-duty rifle

was poised at his hip. Before he could spray bullets, Burke lunged. He tackled Logan, pinning him to the ground on his belly.

A second man came out of the trailer with his hands in the air. "Don't shoot."

The only one who hadn't given up was Logan. He struggled on the ground. The correct protocol would be to cuff him and proceed with standard interrogation, but Burke had a different idea. If Logan thought he had a chance, he'd spill more information.

Purposely, Burke gave him just enough room to scramble to his feet. Logan took off, running toward the barn.

Burke pursued. Though he could have easily overtaken Logan, he stayed one step behind. Just before Logan entered the barn, he grabbed his collar and spun him around. They were face-to-face.

"Where's Nicole?" Burke demanded.

Logan took a wild swing, and Burke allowed the other man's fist to make contact with the Kevlar vest. That had to hurt.

Logan yelled in pain. "Take off your armor. Fight me like a man."

"Give me a reason," Burke said. "Where's Nicole?"

"She was here. But not anymore."

Burke flipped off his helmet. "Your men abducted her by the creek. Right?"

"It was a joke. I was going to let her go."

The cold night air felt good on Burke's face. He was nearly as anxious to take off the protective gear as Logan was to have him do so. He yanked off the arm guards and tossed them aside.

Remembering his training as a negotiator, Burke offered a morsel of hope. "If you're not involved in the kidnapping, this might turn out okay for you."

Except for the murder of Barbara Ayers and the illegal smuggling. But Burke didn't mention those charges. Or the fact that he'd just seen Logan shoot that woman in the leg.

Burke said, "We could make a deal."

Though Logan's eyes were red and watery from the smoke, he brightened. Deal making was his thing.

"It's Butch Thurgood and Pete Richter," he said. "They've got her. They took Nicole to the cave and never came back."

Burke shed his Kevlar vest. His arms and upper body were free. "You asked for half a mil in ransom."

"But I didn't have Nicole. Like I said, just a joke."

"Not very funny."

Burke balanced his weight on the balls of his feet, ready to attack. He laid back and waited for Logan to make the first move. Which he did.

Logan took a jab toward Burke's chin. He missed.

Burke retaliated with a quick body shot—hard enough to double Logan over. "You're working with somebody inside the Carlisle Ranch. Who is it?"

Logan dragged himself upright. "I'm not going to prison, right?"

"Give me a name."

"Lucas Mann. I paid him to help us with the sabotage. He let us know when we could get inside the ranch and make trouble."

Burke feinted right. With his left hand he smacked Logan's left arm. "Lucas wouldn't set fire to the stable."

Logan drew himself together. His posture signaled that he was getting ready for a final assault. But Burke was already thinking three steps ahead. He knew Logan would go for the body, the biggest target. Burke shifted just enough to let Logan's blow crease the outer edge of his ribs.

This negotiation was almost over. Burke shot out with his right fist, shoving Logan's shoulder. "Did Lucas set fire to the barn?"

"He didn't know what we were planning, but he told us a good time to strike. Then the old fool raised the alarm."

Burke ducked another flailing blow and responded with a pop to Logan's face, hard enough to break his handsome nose.

"Where's Nicole?"

"Don't know." Logan wailed. "You busted my nose."

Burke moved closer. "Last chance for you to get out of this. Where is she?"

"If I knew, I'd tell."

Burke believed him. Logan had been double-crossed by his own men. They had taken Nicole to make a big score for themselves. He spun Logan around and cuffed him. "Sam Logan, you're under arrest for the murder of Barbara Ayers. And for illegal smuggling."

Smith ran up beside him. "I have bad news, Burke."

"Now what?"

"Carolyn called Corelli. She's delivering the ransom. At *La Rana*."

Cold dread gripped his heart. There was no more time for strategy or tactics. Carolyn was in danger.

THE STRAP OF THE BACKPACK rubbed against the bruise where Carolyn had been shot. The pain reminded her that Logan wanted her dead. Even though she'd remembered to bring a gun this time, she didn't feel safe. His men had already tried to kill her once; she'd be crazy to ride into the center of the feeding pasture. Sitting erect in the saddle, she couldn't hide.

Throughout her ride from the house, she stayed low, leaning over her horse's neck. At the gate, she slipped to the ground and removed the heavy pack holding a million dollars.

Burke was going to be angry when he found out what she was doing. *Oh, Burke, I'm sorry. If I ever see you again, I'll make it up to you.*

On horseback, Carolyn could have easily maneuvered her way through the herd. But she assumed the kidnapper was close: she had to proceed on foot. She unlatched the gate and stepped inside the enclosure.

She couldn't turn back. Nicole's life was at stake.

Carolyn unlatched the gate and stepped inside. The musky scent from three hundred head of cattle didn't bother her; she'd grown up with that odor. Plenty of hay was strewn across the packed earth; she couldn't worry about where she was stepping or what she was stepping in. The dim moonlight shone on the fat rock formation that looked like a squatting frog. *La Rana.*

The herd seemed to sense that something was wrong. These were mature cattle, nine hundred pounds and up. Restlessly, they stamped their hooves and made nervous noises as if to warn each other of danger.

Using the cattle for cover, she crept closer to the rocks with the pack slung over her good right shoulder and her gun in hand. She didn't want to shoot; the noise could set off a stampede.

She heard a horseman approaching. He yelled, "Carolyn. Where the hell are you?"

Lucas. He'd almost admitted that he was the

traitor. But was he the kidnapper? Was he here to collect the ransom?

She ducked down and said nothing.

"Damn it all," Lucas barked. "I'm on your side. I'm here to help you out."

Help me out of one million dollars? She didn't trust him. Not anymore.

He rode through the gate.

Though she tried to be invisible, he spotted her and approached. She dropped the ransom. Without hesitation, she aimed at the center of his chest. "I don't want to shoot you. Just take the money. And bring Nicole back to us."

"You got it wrong," he said. "When I hooked up with Logan, I thought I was just making some extra cash for letting him play harmless pranks. I didn't know—"

"Kidnapping isn't a prank. It's a federal offense."

"I'd never hurt Nicole. Don't you know that?"

She wanted to believe him. "How did you know to come here?"

"I followed you. When I saw you toting that backpack, I guessed what was going on. That's the ransom, ain't it? What are you fixing to do with it?"

"The instruction was to leave it at *La Rana*."

"Hand it over to me. I'll do it for you."

Or he could ride off with the backpack. If Lucas wasn't the kidnapper, he could botch the ransom delivery. "If you really want to help me, back off."

"At least let me clear a path through these steers."

He rode past her, expertly using his horse to nudge the snorting, frightened cattle out of the way.

Carolyn saw her way clear to *La Rana*. She ran. Dropped the backpack. It was done. She'd fulfilled her part of the bargain.

Leaning against the rocks, she checked her wrist-watch. Less than half an hour had passed since she and Dylan had taken the call from the kidnapper. Very soon, her brother would see his wife again. The nightmare would be over.

"This way," Lucas said.

Dodging a wild-eyed steer, she ran toward Lucas. He seemed to be helping her, forming a barrier between her and the other cattle. She was almost to the fence when she saw him turn in the saddle and glance over his shoulder toward *La Rana*.

"Look out," he yelled. He wheeled his horse around. His rifle was in hand.

Gunfire exploded.

Lucas was slammed out of the saddle.

The herd began to move, shuffling nervously. The gunshot had spooked them.

Carolyn peered through the darkness at the rock formation. The kidnapper was there, hiding like a coward. She raised her gun, ready to shoot if she saw the slightest movement. Firing her weapon while she stood in the midst of the herd was suicide; they'd stampede. But she had to face the son of a bitch—to shoot him before he shot her. Adrenaline pumped through her veins.

He'd have to show himself when he stepped out from behind the rocks to grab the ransom.

Behind her, she heard Lucas moan. *Help him? Or watch for the kidnapper?* Damn it, she couldn't let Lucas die. She lowered her gun and went toward the fallen man.

He was on his hands and knees beside his horse. He was bleeding heavily from a chest wound. "Save yourself."

"You're not dead yet."

Using every bit of her strength, she helped him onto his horse. They were near the fence. Not far from the gate.

Looking back toward *La Rana,* she saw a dark shadow against the rocks. *The kidnapper.* Before she could get her gun ready to shoot, he raised his rifle and fired several shots into the air.

The cattle reacted. Swept up in the rush of heavy flanks and shoulders, she was carried away from the fence, engulfed in the surging mass. She could only hope that Lucas's horse would make it to the gate. And that she would find her way clear.

Shouts filled the air. Peering over the backs of the cattle, she saw cowboys riding toward the field. She thought she recognized Burke's voice. He'd come for her.

The cattle jolted against each other. Three

hundred of them in this field. There wasn't enough room for them to run full out, not unless they broke through the barbed wire. If they stampeded, she didn't have a chance.

She stumbled but didn't fall. Clinging to the side of a massive steer, she was carried forward by his momentum, almost losing her footing. Instead of escaping, she was pushed farther away from the barbed wire fence.

Desperately, she clung to the panicked steer. Another steer banged against her. If she didn't get out of here, she'd be crushed, pounded into the earth by the animals that were her livelihood.

Chapter Twenty-Two

Paying no attention to the warnings from cowboys who knew better, Burke rode through the gate into the mass of cattle. Being trampled was one hell of a way to die. He had to reach Carolyn.

He saw her. She clung desperately to a giant steer. He nudged his horse forward, glad that his mount was more experienced than he was.

Carolyn darted toward him. With one arm, he reached down and lifted her off the ground. She was in his arms, safely cradled against him.

In seconds, he was at the gate.

Outside the barbed wire fence, Burke held her close. He was still astride his horse so it wasn't the most comfortable position. But he didn't care. His arms clamped around her.

"Burke, you can put me down."

"Never."

The other cowboys who rode with him to *La Rana*

were busy, getting the herd inside the fence under control and rescuing the man who'd been shot.

He kissed Carolyn's sweaty forehead. She didn't exactly smell like a rose garden, but he was happy to be near her, grateful that she was safe.

She turned her face up to look at him. Smears of grime marred her pale cheeks and forehead. Her hat was gone. Her black hair tangled like a bird's nest. She'd never been so beautiful.

"I'm sorry," she said. "You told me not to leave the house without you."

"It doesn't matter who's right and who's wrong." He was in no mood for negotiating or competition. "You're safe. That's the important thing."

"We got a phone call from the kidnapper. And from Nicole. She told Dylan that—"

"Nicole? You're sure it was her?"

"Dylan recognized her voice, and he ought to know. She told him to meet her at the creek. She'd be there after the ransom was delivered here. So Dylan and I split up to handle both things. That must mean there are two kidnappers."

"Butch Thurgood and Pete Richter," he said. "Logan already ratted them out."

"Did you rescue the women and children at the compound?"

"Worked out as planned. Logan is in custody." He needed to step up and take charge of the operation again. "Before I get back to business, there's something I need to tell you."

A brave smile twitched her lips. "Do you mean I have your undivided attention? For the next two minutes?"

"Forever," he said. "You will always have my undivided attention. Carolyn, you're the center of my universe."

Her green eyes widened. "I am?"

"You look surprised."

"Oh, yeah. I definitely am. Stunned, even."

In a way, he was amazed, too. They'd only known each other for a couple of days, and he wasn't generally given to emotional outbursts. "I love you, Carolyn."

She wrapped her arms around his neck and kissed him hard. He loved her passion. Her strength. Her character.

She whispered, "I love you, too."

For a moment they stared into each other's eyes, basking in the strange glow of this shocking discovery. *They were in love, capital L-O-V-E.*

MacKenzie rode up beside them. His face was somber. "Lucas didn't make it."

"I'm sorry," Carolyn said in a measured tone. "He died trying to save my life."

If she didn't want to condemn him, Burke wouldn't refute her. Lucas had died and there was no reason to tarnish his good reputation. "Carolyn, where did you drop the ransom?"

"On the rocks."

He snapped off an order, "MacKenzie, go to those rocks in the center of the field. Look for a backpack."

"Backpack?"

"You heard him," Carolyn said. "A huge backpack full of money. A million dollars in cash."

The young man blinked. "Holy crap."

"Go," Burke ordered.

While he took out his cell phone, Carolyn repositioned herself so she was sitting in front of him on the saddle. He contacted Corelli and told him where Dylan was headed.

He hoped there would be a happy ending for all of them, that Dylan would ride back to the ranch with Nicole. He wrapped his arms around Carolyn's slender waist. "Do you want to ride back on your own horse?"

"Not really." She snuggled against him. "I used to be so concerned about appearances, worried that the ranch hands wouldn't respect me if I showed weakness or emotion."

"Unless they're blind and deaf, I'm pretty sure they know something's going on between us."

"Do you think so?"

He'd spent last night in her bed, and they hadn't exactly been silent. "They know."

As she rested against him, they watched the cowboys climbing over *La Rana,* searching every crevice. MacKenzie waved both arms. "It's not here."

The ransom was gone. Burke had expected as much. Butch and Richter had figured out a simple but clever drop point. All they had to do to create a diversion was fire a gun and get out of the way while the stampeding herd covered their escape. "What happened when Lucas was shot?"

"I had made the drop, and I was trying to get out of the field. He rode ahead of me, clearing a path. Then, he turned in the saddle and spotted something behind me."

"On *La Rana?*"

"Yes," she said. "Lucas didn't have time to pull his rifle before they opened fire. Lucas was the traitor."

"I know."

"But he admitted that he'd made a mistake." She exhaled a shuddering breath. "I want to remember the good things about him."

It was hard to believe Logan had no part in this operation, but he clearly hadn't expected the raid on the compound. Additionally, the FBI team with the chopper had taken the smugglers on the Indian Trail into custody. "When we get back to the ranch, it's going to be chaos. There will be hostages to process. And a mob of FBI to deal with."

"There's only one thing I'm worried about," she said.

"Me?" he asked hopefully.

She twisted her head to kiss his neck. "Do I need to worry about you?"

"Not really. I know where I stand."

"Where's that, Burke?"

"At your side. As long as you'll have me."

"That sounds good," she said. "But I wasn't really talking about you. I'm worried about what's happening between Dylan and Nicole. The problems between them run deep. What if she doesn't want to get back together with him?"

"That's her decision."

His job ended when Nicole was released.

As Burke had predicted, the scene at the ranch house was crazy. Every light in the house was lit. Headlights from vans and trucks raced back and forth. There were terse conversations from cowboys and commandos alike.

Carolyn climbed down from the saddle and stood looking up at the man who had saved her life for the second time. The man she loved.

"Go ahead, Burke. I know you have a lot to do. I'm going to the corral to wait for Dylan."

He dismounted. "I'm staying with you."

It felt good to have him put her first. "Aren't there a lot of people you need to be ordering around?"

"They'll manage." He hooked his arm around her waist.

Together, they strolled toward the corral. The horse Burke had been riding trailed behind them. Though the night was far from silent, they seemed to be in their own little bubble of safety—a bubble that could be easily burst if Dylan didn't return to the ranch with his wife.

From across the moonlit field, she spotted her brother riding toward her. Alone.

Her heart skipped a beat. She couldn't be happy in her newfound love if Nicole was...

She ran to meet Dylan.

He dismounted slowly.

"I saw her," he said. "We talked."

"Is she all right?" Carolyn asked. "Where is she?"

"Not with me. Not anymore." He held out his open palm, showing her the wedding ring. "Nicole isn't coming back to me. She wants a divorce."

Carolyn took the ring and read the inscription: My horizon. *This couldn't be true.* "I don't believe—"

"Believe it," he said. "My horizon. My ass. The sun has set. She doesn't love me anymore."

There had been hints. When Carolyn first showed up at the ranch, Nicole hadn't wanted to talk. Not that they'd had many conversations lately. Carolyn had been too busy, hadn't expected to encounter a problem like this. A divorce.

"Your wife picked a hell of a way to break up with you," Burke said. "Was the kidnapping staged?"

"No."

She searched her brother's face for a clue. He wore a stern mask to hide his pain and humiliation. "I want some answers, Dylan. Why did she keep signaling us that she was at the Circle M?"

"We didn't talk about that. She told me that being kidnapped was a blessing in disguise. It gave her time to think."

"I want to talk to her." Carolyn needed to see for herself, wanted to hear the words from Nicole's lips.

"That's why she's not coming back to the ranch. Doesn't want to explain herself to anybody." He gestured to the ranch house where teams of FBI and cowboys hustled in and out. "It's over. All these damn people can go back to where they came from."

"Sorry," Burke said. "But that's not how this type of investigation works. I need to be sure the victim is all right."

"She's well." Dylan spat the words. "The only thing wrong is that…she's gone."

Carolyn pressed, "Tell me her exact words."

"None of your business. This is between me and my wife." He straightened his shoulders. "My ex-wife."

"What about the ransom?" Burke asked.

"Money well spent," Dylan said, "if it means I'm done with her. I'm calling off the investigation. Nicole isn't a missing person. Nobody was holding a gun to her head. She's leaving of her own accord."

He turned his back and walked slowly toward the barn. Though his posture was erect and stoic, Carolyn knew that he was falling apart inside. And so was she. Her brief moment of happiness seemed to be crumbling. "Do something, Burke."

"Legally, I can't track down a person who isn't missing."

"You've picked a fine time to play by the rules." Her hand closed around the wedding band. "Can't you make Nicole come back? Make her explain to me."

Her gaze searched his face, looking for a reason to hope that this would turn out.

"I won't lie to you." His dark eyes shone in the night. He kissed her forehead. "Dylan is satisfied that Nicole is well. I don't have the authority to pursue further investigation."

"But I'm not satisfied." This wasn't the happy ending she'd hoped for. "Dylan might be willing to write off a million dollars, but I'm not. I want the ransom back."

"Good point."

Nicole had simple tastes. She wasn't the sort of

woman who needed a million dollars to start a new life. "I can't believe she took the money."

"That might have been the price the kidnappers required. The price of her freedom."

"It's just not right."

"I won't leave you alone to handle this," he said. "The kidnapping is over but I'm staying here. I won't abandon you, Carolyn."

"Thank you." She clung to him, needing him more than ever. "You just keep saving my life, over and over."

"That's my job."

Never before did she have someone to lean on, someone to share the burden. And she was going to need his continued support, especially during the next few days. He was her rock, her strength, her one true love.

* * * * *

Cassie Miles continues
CHRISTMAS AT THE CARLISLES'
next month. Don't miss
BODYGUARD UNDER THE MISTLETOE,
only from
Harlequin Intrigue®!

*Celebrate 60 years of pure reading pleasure
with Harlequin®!*

To commemorate the event, Silhouette Special
Edition invites you to Ashley O'Ballivan's
bed-and-breakfast in the small town of Stone
Creek. The beautiful innkeeper will have her
hands full caring for her old flame Jack
McCall. He's on the run and recovering from
a mysterious illness, but that won't stop him
from trying to win Ashley back.

*Enjoy an exclusive glimpse of Linda Lael Miller's
AT HOME IN STONE CREEK
Available in November 2009
from Silhouette Special Edition®.*

The helicopter swung abruptly sideways in a dizzying arch, setting Jack McCall's fever-ravaged brain spinning.

His friend's voice sounded tinny, coming through the earphones. "You belong in a hospital," he said. "Not some backwater bed-and-breakfast."

All Jack really knew about the virus raging through his system was that it wasn't contagious, and there was no known treatment for it besides a lot of rest and quiet. "I don't like hospitals," he responded, hoping he sounded like his normal self. "They're full of sick people."

Vince Griffin chuckled but it was a dry sound, rough at the edges. "What's in Stone Creek, Arizona?" he asked. "Besides a whole lot of nothin'?"

Ashley O'Ballivan was in Stone Creek, and she was a whole lot of somethin', but Jack had neither the strength nor the inclination to explain. After the way he'd ducked out six months before, he didn't expect a welcome, knew he didn't deserve one. But Ashley, being Ashley, would take him in whatever her misgivings.

He had to get to Ashley; he'd be all right.

He closed his eyes, letting the fever swallow him.

There was no telling how much time had passed when he became aware of the chopper blades slowing overhead. Dimly, he saw the private ambulance waiting on the airfield outside of Stone Creek; it seemed that twilight had descended.

Jack sighed with relief. His clothes felt clammy against his flesh. His teeth began to chatter as two figures unloaded a gurney from the back of the ambulance and waited for the blades to stop.

"Great," Vince remarked, unsnapping his seat belt. "Those two look like volunteers, not real EMTs."

The chopper bounced sickeningly on its runners, and Vince, with a shake of his head, pushed open his door and jumped to the ground, head down.

Jack waited, wondering if he'd be able to stand on his own. After fumbling unsuccessfully with the buckle on his seat belt, he decided not.

When it was safe the EMTs approached, following Vince, who opened Jack's door.

His old friend Tanner Quinn stepped around Vince, his grin not quite reaching his eyes.

"You look like hell warmed over," he told Jack cheerfully.

"Since when are you an EMT?" Jack retorted.

Tanner reached in, wedged a shoulder under Jack's right arm and hauled him out of the chopper. His knees immediately buckled, and Vince stepped up, supporting him on the other side.

"In a place like Stone Creek," Tanner replied, "everybody helps out."

They reached the wheeled gurney, and Jack found himself on his back.

Tanner and the second man strapped him down, a process that brought back a few bad memories.

"Is there even a hospital in this place?" Vince asked irritably from somewhere in the night.

"There's a pretty good clinic over in Indian Rock," Tanner answered easily, "and it isn't far to Flagstaff." He paused to help his buddy hoist Jack and the gurney into the back of the ambulance. "You're in good hands, Jack. My wife is the best veterinarian in the state."

Jack laughed raggedly at that.

Vince muttered a curse.

Tanner climbed into the back beside him, perched on some kind of fold-down seat. The other man shut the doors.

"You in any pain?" Tanner said as his partner climbed into the driver's seat and started the engine.

"No." Jack looked up at his oldest and closest friend and wished he'd listened to Vince. Ever since he'd come down with the virus—a week after snatching a five-year-old girl back from her non-custodial parent, a small-time Colombian drug dealer—he hadn't been able to think about anyone or anything but Ashley. When he *could* think, anyway.

Now, in one of the first clearheaded moments he'd experienced since checking himself out of Bethesda the day before, he realized he might be making a major mistake. Not by facing Ashley—he owed her that much and a lot more. No, he could be putting her in danger, putting Tanner and his daughter and his pregnant wife in danger, too.

"I shouldn't have come here," he said, keeping his voice low.

Tanner shook his head, his jaw clamped down hard as though he was irritated by Jack's statement.

"This is where you belong," Tanner insisted. "If you'd had sense enough to know that six months ago, old buddy, when you bailed on Ashley without so much as a fare-thee-well, you wouldn't be in this mess."

Ashley. The name had run through his mind a million times in those six months, but hearing somebody say it out loud was like having a fist close around his insides and squeeze hard.

Jack couldn't speak.

Tanner didn't press for further conversation.

The ambulance bumped over country roads, finally hitting smooth blacktop.

"Here we are," Tanner said. "Ashley's place."

* * * * *

Will Jack be able to
patch things up with Ashley,
or will his past put the woman he loves
in harm's way?
Find out in
AT HOME IN STONE CREEK
by Linda Lael Miller
Available November 2009
from Silhouette Special Edition®.

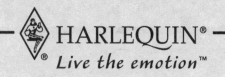

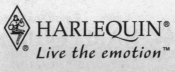

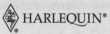

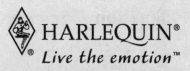

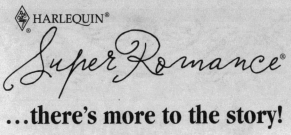

HARLEQUIN®

Super Romance®

...there's more to the story!

Superromance.
A *big* satisfying read about unforgettable
characters. Each month we offer *six* very different
stories that range from family drama to adventure
and mystery, from highly emotional stories to
romantic comedies—and much more! Stories
about people you'll believe in and care about.
Stories too compelling to put down....

Our authors are among today's *best* romance
writers. You'll find familiar names and talented
newcomers. Many of them are award winners—
and you'll see why!

If you want the biggest and best
in romance fiction, you'll get it
from Superromance!

Exciting, Emotional, Unexpected...

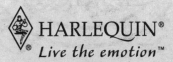

HARLEQUIN®

Live the emotion™

Harlequin® Historical
Historical Romantic Adventure!

Imagine a time of chivalrous knights and unconventional ladies, roguish rakes and impetuous heiresses, rugged cowboys and spirited frontierswomen— these rich and vivid tales will capture your imagination!

Harlequin Historical . . . they're too good to miss!

HHDIR06

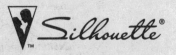